Remembering

A NOVEL BY

Wendell Berry

NORTH POINT PRESS
San Francisco 1988

I am grateful to Bucknell University for inviting me to be
Poet-in-Residence in the winter of 1987. Much of the
work on this book was done during that time.

The events of this book are imaginary, and none of its
characters is intended to represent any actual person.

For Ed and Cia McClanahan

. . . to him that is joined to
all the living there is hope . . .

Ecclesiastes 9:4

Let the fragments of love be reassembled in
you. Only then will you have true courage.

Hayden Carruth

Heavenly Muse, Spirit who brooded on
The world and raised it shapely out of nothing,
Touch my lips with fire and burn away
All dross of speech, so that I keep in mind
The truth and end to which my words now move
In hope. Keep my mind within that Mind
Of which it is a part, whose wholeness is
The hope of sense in what I tell. And though
I go among the scatterings of that sense,
The members of its worldly body broken,
Rule my sight by vision of the parts
Rejoined. And in my exile's journey far
From home, be with me, so I may return.

Remembering

I.

Darkness Visible

It is dark. He does not know where he is. And then he sees pale light from the street soaking in above the drawn drapes. It is not a light to see by, but only makes the darkness visible. He has slept, to his surprise, but has wakened in the same unease that kept him sleepless long after he went to bed and that remained with him in dream.

In his dream a great causeway had been built across the creek valley where he lives, the heavy roadbed and its supports a materialized obliviousness to his house and barn that stood belittled nearby, as if great Distance itself had come to occupy that place. Bulldozers pushed and trampled the loosened, disformed, denuded earth, working it like dough toward some new shape entirely human-conceived. The place was already unrecognizable except for the small house and barn destined to be enrubbled with all the rest that had been there. Watching, Andy knew that all the last remnants of old forest, the chief beauty and dignity of that place, were now fallen and gone. The flowers that had bloomed in the shade of the standing groves in the spring were gone. The birds were gone. The fields and their names, the farmsteads and the neighbors were gone; the graveyards and the names of the dead, all gone.

So near to the causeway as to be almost under it stood a concrete building of long, windowless, humming corridors, in which workers were passing. In the depths of the building, in a blank-walled, whitely lighted room, a fat man sat behind a desk, eating the living flesh of his own forearm, all the while making a speech in a tone of pleading reasonableness:

"I *have* to do this. I am *starving*. Three meals a day are *not* enough. To get more, it would be necessary to contract unsavory foreign alliances. I cannot *afford* to quit. I realize that this is not ideal. But I am not an idealist. I am not a naive dreamer. I am constrained by my circumstances to be a hard-headed realist. Neighbors? I have no neighbors. Friends? I have no friends. This is my independence. This is my victory."

The causeway, the labyrinthine building, the house and barn, all the diminished, naked valley, were dim in midday dusk, the dingy light too weak to cast a shadow.

An old terror, learned long ago from his time, returned to Andy now and shook him—not the terror of the end of the world, but of the end, simply, of all he knew and loved, which would then exist only in his knowing, the little creature of his memory, and so he would be forced to collaborate willy-nilly in the dominance of human intention over the world.

But he knew that he was already implicated, already one of the guilty, for as he looked upon that destroyed place, which once had been his home, he realized that even as he mourned it he could not remember it as it was; he could find in his spirit no vision of anything it ever was that it ever might be again. For he himself had been diminished. He himself was disformed and naked, a mere physical quantity, its existence verifiable by an ache. That is what woke him.

As he lies in bed in the dark room, only his mind is awake, his body feelingless and still. Leaving the dream, as a place to which it may return again, his mind resumes a thoughtless, exhausted wakefulness, dumbly pained. The unhanded, healed stump of his right wrist lies in the dark beside him. For the time, he is refusing to think about it, though that refusal costs him all thought.

But thought comes. His body twitches and stirs on its own, alerts itself to the strangeness of bed and room, and absence lives again at the end of his arm.

The feel of the bed, the smell of the room seem compounded of the strangeness of all the strangers who have slept there: salesmen, company officers, solitary travelers, who have entered, shut the door, set down their bags, and stood, weary and silent, afraid to speak, even to themselves, their own names. A man could go so far from home, he thinks, that his own name would become unspeakable by him, unanswerable by anyone, so that if he dared to speak it, it would escape him utterly, a bird out an open window, leaving him untongued in some boundless amplitude of mere absence.

It is as though his name is now a secret, a small vital organ pulsing its life away. For now he has come to a place where no one knows his name but himself, where nobody but himself knows where he is. He is still going away on the far side of the boundary he crossed when he came up the ramp at the airport and saw the young woman whose name and description he carried in a letter in his pocket. She stood amid the crowd, looking for him this way and that around the heads and shoulders of the unloading passengers who hurried past, dividing around her. She saw him and smiled, anxiety leaving her face. She was from the college where, in two hours, he was to speak.

"Pardon me. Are you Andrew Catlett?"

He looked at her as if surprised to be so accosted, and stepped past.

"No mam."

He had come to San Francisco from an agriculture conference held that day at a great university of the Midwest. The meeting had taken place in a low building of cast concrete, of which the second story was much wider than the first, as if an architect unable to draw a curve had attempted to design a large mushroom. The walls inside were also of concrete, left unfinished. In contrast to the rude walls, all the appointments of the interior were luxurious: the stair rails of polished mahogany, the draperies richly woven, the carpets so bright and soft that the conferees moving over them made no sound, as if treading on clouds. The second-floor lobby, surrounded by meeting rooms, was furnished with deep-cushioned chairs and sofas; a table with a white cloth bore a coffee urn and an assortment of pastries. The effect of these rich furnishings, the silence of the carpet, and the correspondingly hushed voices of the conferees standing in groups, was that of bated anticipation; the room seemed not to have accepted those who were in it, but to remain expectant of someone more important who perhaps was not going to attend.

As the time of the meeting drew near, the conferees moved to the white-clothed table, set down their empty cups, and singly and in groups straggled into the meeting room. Andy, who did not know anyone, took a seat high up in the back. The room was a large theater, with many rows of seats steeply pitched toward a dais at the front. On the dais was a lectern with a microphone in front of a huge blank screen. The room was windowless, lighted with bright, cold light. The fan of a distant air conditioner whispered through the walls.

Having come in just at starting time from the clear warm morning outdoors, Andy felt suddenly submerged, as if he were sitting on the bottom of an aquarium. That his ears were still tightly stopped from his plane flight seemed to corroborate this impression with physical evidence. It was as though he had changed, not only elements, but worlds. Where was he only this morning?

He got up in the dark, the whole country asleep around him in the stillness at four o'clock. He went to the barn, did the feeding and milking, and returned to the house where Flora had his breakfast waiting. He went in sheepishly, for they had quarreled the night before and he had not succeeded in shedding the blame for it, not even in his own eyes. But she said "Good morning" brightly, and took the milk bucket from him with a smile.

He wanted impulsively to tell her how slow and awkward he still felt, choring with one hand, but he held himself back. He had told her, Heaven knew, often enough, for much of his thought now had to do with the comparison of times, as if he were condemned forever to measure the difference between his life when he was whole and his life now. He told her, instead, "Good morning," and then, reaching toward her as she turned away, "Listen, Flora, I *hate* to quarrel with you."

She turned back, smiling, determined, he saw, to be superior to the possibility of yet another quarrel. "Then why do you do it?"

He had hoped, vaguely, for some reconciliation between them. And so he did not say as he might have said, not in justice, but to prolong the contest, the contact, "Well, why do you quarrel with me?" There was not time for that, and he felt hollowed out by his anger of the night before. He said, "Wait. Listen. Are the children up?"

"No."

"Well, listen. I don't like to leave, feeling the way I do."

She answered him in the light-hearted, practical tone that always infuriated him, as she undoubtedly knew. "When the time comes to leave you have to leave, I suppose, and how you feel doesn't matter. How *do* you feel?"

Again the anger flashed in him that would leave him burnt and empty in his soul. "You know goddamned well how I feel."

He had the satisfaction of seeing her lips tighten. She was straining the milk, not looking at him.

"Oh," she said. "Well, if you say so. It's lovely that you understand me so well."

"I feel like I'm no account to anybody."

"Well, unfortunately, that's not for you to decide. Have you asked me? Have you asked the children? Have you asked Nathan or Henry or Wheeler or your mother?"

He started to raise his right forearm in a gesture, as if the hand were still attached, and then caught himself and put the hook behind him. "*Why* should you want to live with me?"

Even in his anger he knew that he was pleading with her, hoping to be surprised by a better reason than he knew.

"Oh, I guess because I'm used to you. Sort of."

She had put the strained milk into the refrigerator and now was at the sink, rinsing the bucket, wiping it out with the dishrag.

"Flora, you don't love me. You never have."

She stood looking at him, holding the dishrag in her hand. And then she flung it hard into his face.

He can still feel the lick, as if it is burned onto his skin. Lying in the strange room in the dark, he can feel it. And he can see the look she gave him afterwards, surprised at herself, perhaps, as he certainly had been, but determined too. He saw that he had met finality in her, and he understood it. She was *done* with him as he had become. There was nothing for him to do but change his clothes and go.

She did not look at him again. She did not leave the kitchen. She did not call out to him any word at all. And he said nothing to her. When he shut the door behind him, the children were not awake.

His anger flickers in him again. She will not have him as he is, and he will not crawl back to her through the needle's eye of her demand.

Now he is outside whatever held them together. He feels the vastness of that exterior, but it does not excite him as he wishes. Would there be in all the boundlessness of it another woman, perhaps more than one other, another kind of life, for such a man as himself?

It does not excite him. It is only where he is.

A man with somewhat disheveled hair and a worried look came to the rostrum, removed the worried look from his face as if suddenly aware that he stood in public, and smiled warmly at the clock on the back wall of the room.

"We appear at last to have reached the beginning of our conference, 'The Future of the American Food System.'"

He introduced himself as a member of the Department of Agricultural Economics and one of the organizers of the conference. He expressed his deep conviction of the importance of the conference in this our Bicentennial Year, quoting, in support, words of a high agricultural official to the effect that "man can live without petroleum, but not without food." He said that he supposed we had to have *some* petroleum in order to produce food but that, anyhow, we could not eat petroleum. He said that he was an old farm boy himself, and understood from firsthand experience the problems of America's food producers and also their indispensible contribution to the economy of our country and indeed of the world.

He then said that he felt highly honored to present the first speaker of the day, the high agricultural official just quoted, in fact, who was an old farm boy who had made good, by becoming, first, a professor of agriculture, and then a great administrator in a great college of agriculture, and then the chairman of the board of a great agribusiness firm, and then an agricultural official, and then a high agricultural official.

The professor sat down. The high official stood and, amid much respectful applause, made his way to the rostrum. His dark suit was as unwrinkled as if made of steel. He was faultlessly groomed. He was a man completely in charge of his face, on which not the slightest smile or frown might appear without his permission. Or he was completely in charge of his face except for his left eye which, while his right eye looked at his notes or the audience, gazed about on its own.

"Thank you," he said. "I have thought that perhaps it is inappropriate for me to speak at the beginning of this conference, the title of which implies that there may be some question or problem about the future of the American food system, and I can only reassure you: The American food system is going to continue to be, because it is, one of the wonders of the modern world."

Andy, sitting in the back row with Flora's lick angry on his face, shrugged it away in response to pain from another adversary. He took from his jacket pocket a small notebook, opened it, and wrote, "Am Fd Syst. Wndr of mdrn wrld." After months of enforced practice, his left hand was finally learning to write at moderate speed a script that was moderately legible. But it was still a child's script that he wrote, bearing not much resemblance to the work of his late right hand. That had flowed like flight almost, looping and turning without his consciousness, as if by intelligence innate in itself. This goes by rude twists and angles, with unexpected jerks, the hand responding grudgingly to his orders, seized with little fits of reluctance.

"I thank my stars," the high official said, "that I grew up a farm boy, and had the opportunity to work closely with my father. I learned some things then that I have never forgotten, and that have stood me in good stead.

"But let's face it. Those days are gone, and their passing is not to be regretted. A lot of you here are old farm boys, and you know what I mean. You knew what it was to look all day at the north end of a southbound horse. You knew what it was to walk that outhouse path on a zero night. Your mothers and sisters knew what it was to stand over a hot wood stove when it was a hundred degrees, and no air conditioning.

"I, for one, don't want to go back to those days. I'm glad you can't turn back the clock. I want to live in a changing, growing, dynamic society. I want to go forward with progress into a better future."

Andy wrote, "Lvd wrk. No rtrn. Lvs ftr."

"When I was a boy," the high official said, "forty-five percent of our people were on the farm. Now we have reduced that to about four percent. Millions of people have been released from farmwork to make automobiles and TV sets and plumbing fixtures—in other words, to make this the greatest industrial nation the world has ever seen. Millions of people have been freed from groveling in the earth so that they can now pursue the finer things of life.

"And the four percent left on the farm live better than the forty-five percent ever hoped to live. This four percent we may think of as the permanent staff of this great food production machine that is the farms and fields of America. These people have adapted to the fact that American agriculture is big business. They are as savvy financially as bankers. And they are enjoying the amenities of life— color TV, automobiles, indoor toilets, vacations in Florida or Arizona.

"Oh, I know there are some trade-offs involved in this. There is some breakdown in the old family unit we used to have. The communities are not what they were. I see some small businesses closing down. Farmers have fewer neighbors than they used to have. We have some problems with soil erosion and water shortages and chemical pollution. But that's the price of progress.

"Let me tell you something. This is economics we're talking about. And the basic law of economics is: Adapt or die. Get big or get out. Sure, not everybody is going to make it. But then, not everybody is *supposed* to make it. This is the way a dynamic free-market economy *works*. This is the American system.

"I'm telling you one of the greatest success stories you have ever listened to. The American farmer is now feeding himself and seventy other people. And he can feed the world. He has put in the hands of our government the most powerful weapon it has ever held. I am talking about food."

Andy wrote: "4%. Grvlng in rth. Big biz. Amnty of lf: TV. Trdoffs: fam, cmmnty, nghbrs, soil, wtr. Prc of prg. Adpt or die. Gt bg or gt out. Fr mkt. 1 to 70. Fd wrld. Weapon."

The audience sat submerged in the bright sea-space of the room, the air conditioner pulsing in the walls, the high official's confident, dryly intoned sentences riding over them, wave after wave.

Andy thought, "Why did they invite me?" But he guessed he knew: because he had achieved a certain notoriety for contrary opinions. He was there to inject a note of controversy into the proceedings.

He is a man, he thinks, of contrary opinions—a man the size of a few contrary opinions. In the simple darkness, far away, he no longer feels the uneasiness, the fear indeed, that tightened him in that meeting room. He is afraid, but not of the rostrum, not of any answer anyone might make to anything he might say. What he is afraid of now has not answered.

He raises his right forearm, its lightness still residing in it as if by permanent surprise. The memory comes to him, rising out of the flesh of his arm, of how it felt to flex and then extend the fingers of his right hand. He longs for the release of that movement. As sometimes happens, his hand seems now not to be gone, but caught, unable to move, as if inside an iron glove.

In October they had been helping Jack Penn harvest his corn: Andy and Nathan Coulter and Danny Branch. Jack's father, Elton, had died in the late winter, and Jack, who was twenty-two, had never farmed on his own apart from his father's experience and judgment. And so the three of them, his father's friends, and his, had gone through the whole crop year with him, accepting his help in return for theirs. Now the harvest was almost over. If they could keep everything going until night, they would finish the field. Andy was running the picker, the other three hauling the loaded wagons to the crib and unloading them. They had, in fact, more help than they needed; it was brilliant warmish fall weather, ideal for the job; and today, with the end in sight, they had worked with an ease of mind that they all had enjoyed. Still, because it was getting on in the day with plenty left to do, there was some pressure on the tractor driver to hurry.

The picker became fouled as it had been doing off and on all afternoon, and Andy stopped to clear it, leaving it running. He began pulling the crammed stalks out of the machine, irritated by the delay. He pulled them out one at a time, shucked the ears that were on them, and threw the stalks aside. And then something happened that he thought he had imagined but, as it turned out, had not imagined at all: The machine took his hand. Of course, he knew he must have given the hand, but it was so quickly caught he could almost believe that the machine had leapt for it. While his mind halted, unable to come to the fact, his body fended for itself, braced against the pull, and held. When intelligence lighted in him again, he saw that only the hand was involved, and he carefully shifted his feet so as to give himself more leverage against the rollers; he did not want his jacket sleeve to be caught. And he was already yelling—*Hey! Hey!*—trying to pitch his voice above the noise of the machine.

There is no way for him to know how long he held out against the pull of the rollers, which soon pulled with less force, for they were lubricated with his blood. He was there long enough, anyhow, for the horror of his predicament to become steady, almost habitual, in his mind, although it retained the shock and force of its sudden onset. He heard the long persistence of the noise of the machine that did not know the difference between a cornstalk and a man's arm. He felt its relentless effort to pull him into itself, while the bloodied rollers wore against flesh and crushed bone, and the oblivious metal rattled and shook. He heard his cries to the other men go out time and again.

Finally they must have heard him, for he saw them coming, not with the tractor and empty wagon, but in Nathan's truck. He saw them coming along not too fast, until they saw him and suddenly sped up, the old truck leaping and swaying across the harvested rows.

He saw Jack leap out of the truck before it stopped, run to the tractor, and turn the ignition off. He heard the silence coming slowly down, and Nathan, running, saying to Danny, "Get my toolbox!"

And then they were with him, Danny holding him, his arms

around him, while Jack and Nathan tied a tourniquet above his wrist and then worked to loosen the rollers. When what was left of the hand was ready to come free, Danny clamped his own hand over Andy's eyes.

"Andy," Nathan said, "we've got to get you into the truck now. Don't look at that hand, do you hear? Just keep your eyes shut. We're going to help you."

"All right," Andy said. His voice breaking, he said, "Shoo!" He began to shake. The silence around him rang, the air traveled by flashes and whirls, the day outside him, beyond him, uncannily bright.

By the time he was ready for the operating room, Flora was there. She smiled and picked up his left hand in hers and patted it. She seemed still to be living in that other time, before. "What have you done to yourself?"

Bitterness and fear and shame rushing upon him then, he said, "I've ruined my hand."

His forearm raised as if to lift his open hand to the air, to learn the temperature of it, he lies in the dark, listening. The city around him has subsided to a remote hum, constant and unregarded as the breath of a sleeper. Only once in a while there is the sound of a solitary car moving in the street below.

He is long past sleep now. His mind has begun to work on the agenda that it sets for itself, and he knows that he will not be able to stop it. It is hunting, as if for a way out, and yet is fascinated by every obstacle. He offers it one of his contrary opinions, as he might offer a bone to a dog, and his mind, like a disobedient dog, takes it, tastes it, lets it fall, and continues with its own business. It intends to sniff its way through the Future of the American Food System until it finds the ache in it.

After the high official's speech there was a bustle while he made his exit from the meeting, surrounded by handshakers and thankers. The audience drew its attention back to itself in vague underwater stirring and murmuring until the door to the lobby shut upon the official exit and the organizer of the conference returned to the rostrum to introduce the next speaker: an old farm boy who had become one of the most astute agricultural economists in the world today, whose accomplishments had been universally recognized, and whose services had been found useful by many governments both domestic and foreign.

The great agricultural economist then gravely assumed the rostrum. Like his predecessor, he was impeccably clad, a tall man in a dark brown suit, with a face prepared to be consulted by the government. He beamed upon the audience a moment by way of greeting, adjusted his spectacles, and began to read statistics from a paper:

In the slightly more than a quarter century from 1950 to the present bicentennial year, the tonnage of fertilizer used on American farms increased by 500 percent. During the same period, work hours required in farming decreased by 69 percent, tractor horsepower increased by 149 percent, and the number of tractors by 30 percent. Simultaneously, the farm population declined from 23 million to 7.8 million, a difference of 15.2 million. The number of farms decreased to about half the number in 1950 (from 5.4 to 2.7 million), whereas the average farm size had doubled (from 200 to 400 acres).

These figures, the economist said, were causing concern in some quarters that the family farm might disappear, along with the family's traditional role in farming and other traditions of American agriculture. On the other hand, larger and more efficient farms would provide a larger volume of farm commodities at lower prices and, at the same time, provide a higher standard of living for the remaining farmers.

Obviously, he said, we have a choice to make—or, perhaps, a choice that we have already made. In order to facilitate this choosing, or this acceptance of a choice, as the case might be, the economist and his colleagues had developed a quantimetric model of the American food system.

"The model," he said, "has pre-input, input, and output divisions for each of its fifteen crop submodels." The economist read in a detached monotone, as if thinking of something else.

Andy wrote: "15.2 mlln gone. Qntmtrc mdl. Pre-inpt, inpt, outpt. Submdl." He could see bubbles rising from the great economist's mouth, breaking, high up, in the wash of the light. The economist looked almost as far away as he sounded, far off through the water, his words popping out of the bubbles and sinking back into the room:

"A model will be recursive in structure when two conditions prevail: the matrix of coefficients of endogenous variables must be triangular, and the variance-covariance matrix of structural equation disturbances must be diagonal."

The pencil fell out of Andy's hand, and he leaned and picked it up. His mind was coming loose from his body, beginning to float. It soared upward slowly and, looking down, saw a large green fish give the economist a kiss just under his right eye.

Andy's head fell forward and he woke. He sat up and shook his head. He felt like a sentinel on watch, a mourner at a wake—aggrieved, endangered, and falling asleep.

He wiggled his toes and bit the knuckle of his forefinger and looked around at the people in the room: an audience of professors, mostly, so far as he could tell. A few students. He wondered if any farmers were there and knew that it would be surprising if any were.

Plenty of old farm boys, no doubt, but no farmers. Only sons and a few daughters of farmers, their parents' delegates to the Future of the American Food System.

He thought of Elton Penn, that accurate man, in his year-old grave.

The economist said, "The aggregate submodel collects the pre-input and input variables and adds to them the exogenously derived pre-input and input variables for the American food system as a whole."

What would Elton have said about that? He would have said, "If you're going to talk to me, fellow, you'll have to walk."

That was what Old Jack Beechum once said to Andy's grandfather, Mat Feltner, when Mat was trying to impress him with something learned in college. Old Jack stopped and regarded him, his smart nephew, and went on to the barn. "If you're going to talk to me, Mat, you'll have to walk."

Mat had never forgotten it, and neither had any of the rest of the company of friends who inherited the memories of Old Jack and Mat. It had become one of Elton's bywords, one of the many that he kept stored up for emergent occasions. He had said it to Andy a thousand times. When Andy got his mouth running on what Elton classified as a Big Idea and there was work to be done, Elton would give him a look that made Andy remember the words even before Elton said them. And then Elton would say them: "If you're going to talk to me, Andy, you'll have to walk."

Elton's mind had been, in part, a convocation of the voices of predecessors saying appropriate things at appropriate times, talk-shortening sentences or phrases that he spoke to turn attention back to the job or the place or the concern at hand or for the pure pleasure he took in some propriety of remembrance; and he was a good enough mimic that when he recalled a saying its history would come with it. When he would tell Andy, "If you're going to talk to me, you'll have to walk," it would not be just the two of them talking and listening, but Old Jack would be saying it again to Mat, and Mat to his son-in-law, Wheeler, Andy's father, and Wheeler to Elton, and Elton to Andy all the times before; and an old understanding and an old laughter would renew itself then, and be with them.

"And now may we have the lights out and the first slide, please?" the economist said, and the light obediently subdued itself and departed from the room. The great screen came alight with Table I of the Quantimetric Model of the American Food System, dense with numbers.

In the dark Andy saw what he never actually did see, but had seen in his mind many times as clearly as if he had seen it with his eyes.

Elton had not been well, something he pretended nobody knew. But they did know it. His wife, Mary, knew it. Wheeler knew it. Andy and his brother, Henry, knew it. Arthur and Martin Rowanberry knew it. They knew that he needed help with jobs he never had needed help with before. And they knew he was worried about himself.

"If you don't feel good, Elton, go to the doctor," Mary told him. And he said, "I feel all right."

"Go to the doctor," Andy said. "I'll go with you."

"No."

"Why?"

"Because I'm not going to do it."

"Why?"

"Because I'm not sick."

"And you're not stubborn, either."

"That's right," Elton said, grinning big. "I'm not."

But they knew he was sick. And he knew it, though he made a principle of not knowing it.

"You all come over to supper," Mary said to Sarah, Henry's wife. "Elton's down in the dumps and I am too. Come over and cheer us up."

So they went. And it *was* a cheerful meal. They ate, and then sat at the table afterwards, talking about the times, beginning nearly thirty years before, when Henry and Andy had worked sometimes as Elton's hands. They had gone through some hard days together. The work had been complicated always, and sometimes impeded, by the youth and greenness of the boys, by the brotherhood of the brothers, by the friendship of them all. Most of their workdays had ended in simple weariness, but some had ended in coon hunts, some in fish fries, some in furious arguments, one or two in fights.

Among the results were a lot of funny stories, and that night Elton had been telling them, Henry egging him on.

Elton told about Henry and the bumblebees. They had been cleaning the tool shed, and there was a bundle of old grain sacks hanging from a rafter.

"Cut it down," Elton said.

"Sounds like I hear something humming in there," Henry said.

"Ahhhh, take your knife and cut it down!" Elton said. "There's nothing in there."

"I swear I didn't think there was," he said, for the hundredth time, laughing and looking at Henry, who laughed and looked back, for the hundredth time not believing him.

"So I loaned him my knife. He didn't have a knife, of course. Never did have one. Hasn't got one yet. And he cut it down.

"It fell right on his feet. 'Ow!' he said. 'Ow!' He did a little dance, and then ran right out from under his hat. His clothes were just sizzling."

Elton was laughing while he told it, and they all laughed.

"I reckon it's a lot funnier now than it was then."

"A lot," Henry said. "You were running before I even cut the string."

"*Naw*, I wasn't! No *sir*! I was just as surprised as you."

That had been a long time ago, when Henry was about fourteen and Elton not yet thirty. Probably neither of them any longer knew whether Elton had known about the bees or not. But they played out their old game of accusation and denial once more, both enjoying it, both grateful to be in the same story.

Elton pushed back his chair and got up as if to lead the way into the living room.

"Well," he said, "we've had some good times, haven't we?"

He staggered, reached to catch himself, failed. And all that was left of him fell to the floor.

To Andy, Elton's absence became a commanding presence. He was haunted by things he might have said to Elton that would not be sayable again in this world.

That absence is with him now, but only as a weary fact, known but no longer felt, as if by some displacement of mind or heart he is growing absent from it.

It is the absence of everything he knows, and is known by, that surrounds him now.

He is absent himself, perfectly absent. Only he knows where he is, and he is no place that he knows. His flesh feels its removal from other flesh that would recognize it or respond to its touch; it is numb with exile. He is present in his body, but his body is absent.

He does not know what time it is. Nothing has changed since he woke. The darkness is not different, nor is the faint blur of light above the curtained window, nor are the muted night sounds of the streets.

For a long time he has not moved. He lies with his unhanded right forearm upright in the air in the darkness, his body bemused at its own stillness, as if waiting patiently to see how long his strayed mind will take to notice it again.

And now the anger he felt at the conference starts up in him again, for after his fear and grief and boredom it was anger that finally woke him and hardened him against that room. He did not belong there. He did not know anybody who did belong there.

He listened to a paper on "Suggestible Parameters in the Creation of Agricultural Meaning," read by a long-haired man with a weary face, who had never been consulted by a government and who read his paper diffidently, with oddly placed fits of haste, as if aware of the audience's impending boredom or his own; and then another paper on "The Ontology and Epistemology of Agriculture as a Self-Correcting System," read by a woman whose chief business was to keep anyone from viewing the inside of her mouth.

It was endless, Andy thought, a place of eternal hopelessness, where people were condemned to talk forever of what they could not feel or see, old farm boys and old farm girls in the spell of an occult science, speaking in the absence of the living and the dead a language forever unintelligible to anyone but themselves.

And then—it was nearly noon, and a number of the auditors were leaving—he heard himself introduced as "an agricultural journalist who could hardly be said to be complacent about the Future of the American Food System, but whose ideas had attracted some attention—Mr. Andrew Catlett of Fort William, Kentucky."

Andy, getting to his feet, said loudly, "Port!"

The organizer of the conference bent to the microphone again. "I'm sorry. Yes, of course, Mr. Andrew Catlett of *Port* William, Kentucky." He smiled, and the audience laughed, with sympathy for the organizer and in discomfort at Andy's unseemly chauvinism.

Having made one mistake, and knowing it, Andy proceeded directly to another. Instead of the text of the speech he had prepared, he spread on the rostrum the notes he had made on the speeches preceding his.

"What we have heard discussed here this morning," he said, "is an agriculture of the mind. No farmer is here. No farmer has been mentioned. No one who has spoken this morning has worked a day on an actual farm in twenty years, and the reason for that is that none of the speakers *wants* to work on a farm or to be a farmer. The real interest of this meeting is in the academic careerism and the politics and the business of agriculture, and I daresay that most people here, like the first speaker, are proud to have escaped the life and work of farmers, whom they do not admire.

"This room," he said, "it's an image of the minds of the professional careerists of agriculture—a room without windows, filled with artificial light and artificial air, where everything reducible has been reduced to numbers, and the rest ignored. Nothing that you are talking about, and influencing by your talk, is present here, or can be seen from here."

He knew that he was showing his anger, and perhaps the fear under the anger, and perhaps the grief and confusion under the fear. He looked down to steady himself, feeling some blunder, as yet obscure to him, in everything he had said. He looked up at the audience again.

"I don't believe it is well understood how influence flows from enclosures like this to the fields and farms and farmers themselves.

We've been sitting here this morning, hearing about the American food system and the American food producer, the free market, quantimetric models, pre-inputs, inputs, and outputs, about the matrix of coefficients of endogenous variables, about epistemology and parameters—while actual fields and farms and actual human lives are being damaged. The damage has been going on a long time. The fifteen million people who have left the farms since 1950 left because of damage. There was pain in that departure, not shown in any of the figures we have seen. Not felt in this room. And the pain and the damage began a long time before 1950. I want to tell you a story."

He told them how, after the death of Dorie Catlett, his father's mother, he and his father had sorted through all the belongings that she had kept stored in the closets and the dresser drawers of the old house where she had lived as wife and widow for more than sixty years. They went through the old clothes, the quilt pieces, the boxes of buttons, the little coils and balls of saved string. And old papers— they found letters, canceled checks, canceled notes and mortgages, bills and receipts, all neatly tied in bundles with strips of rag. Among these things they found a bill on which the ink had turned brown, stating that in 1906 Marce Catlett's crop had lacked $3.57 of paying the warehouse commission on its own sale.

Neither Andy nor his father had ever seen the bill before, but it was nevertheless familiar to them, for it had been one of the motives of Wheeler Catlett's life, and it would be one of the motives of Andy's. Wheeler remembered the night his father had brought that bill home. His parents tried to disguise their feelings, and Wheeler and his brother pretended not to notice. But they did notice, and they learned, over a long time, what the bill meant. Marce Catlett had carried his year's work to the warehouse and had come home *owing* the warehouse $3.57. And that meant difficulty, it meant discouragement, it meant grief, it meant shame before creditors. And it might have meant ruin. It was a long time before they knew that it did not mean ruin.

On the back of the bill, in some moment of desperation, Dorie Catlett had written, "Oh, Lord, whatever is to become of us?" And then, beneath, as if to correct what she had written already, she wrote: "Out of the depths have I cried unto thee, O Lord."

"I think that bill came out of a room like this," Andy said, "where a family's life and work can be converted to numbers and to some-body else's profit, but the family cannot be seen and its suffering cannot be felt."

He knew then that he had damaged himself. As he had spoken of his grandmother in that room, she had departed from him. He was sweating. His legs had begun to tremble. And yet he still stood at the rostrum, in the harsh light, in his anger, sounding to himself as if he spoke at the bottom of a well.

"I say damn your systems and your numbers and your ideas. I speak for Dorie Catlett and Marce Catlett. I speak for Mat and Margaret Feltner, for Jack Beechum, for Jarrat and Burley Coulter, for Nathan Coulter and Hannah, for Danny and Lyda Branch, for Martin and Arthur Rowanberry, for Elton and Mary and Jack Penn."

As he named them, the dead and the living, they departed from him, leaving him empty, shaking, wet with sweat. The audience, embarrassed, had begun to shift and murmur. He had to get down, away, out of that light and that room.

"In conclusion," he said, "I would like to say that what I have had to say is no more, and is probably less, than what I have had to say."

He hears himself cry out—"Ah!"—and he is standing in the dark.

2.

An Unknown Room

He is standing in the dark, the sound of his outcry so present to him as to be almost palpable, as if he might reach out and put it back in his mouth. Slowly the memory of the meeting room drifts away from him, and the remembered panic of yesterday becomes, without changing, the panic of today.

He cannot see himself. He reaches into the darkness with his left hand, feeling for the lamp. His fingers encounter loudly the shade, and fumble over it and down over the unfamiliar shape of the stem and base, feeling for the switch, and find it. The room, as strange to him as if he had just entered, assembles itself around him: the disheveled bed, the low stands on either side with identical lamps, and over the lamps identical pastel prints of large tulips, identically framed. Against the wall opposite the bed there is a long sideboard with empty drawers, and over it a mirror that reduplicates the duplicate lamps and pictures, the bed, and himself, his right arm stumped off at the wrist, his left hand still on the lamp switch, his hair and underclothes as mussed as the bed.

He stands, looking at himself in the room in the mirror as though

he is his own disembodied soul. When he'd answered, "No mam,"
to the young woman waiting to meet him at the airport gate, he had
felt the sudden swing and stagger of disembodiment, as though a
profound divorce had occurred, casting his body off to do what it
would on its own, to be watched as from a distance, without pre-
monition of what it might do. And what of that young woman? He
is going to be sorry for his lie to her. He is standing so still that he
might be looking at himself, stuffed, behind glass: "*Homo Ameri-
canus*, c. 1976, perhaps from a border state." And then he sees the
image grimace in dismissal of itself or its onlooker and turn away.

He turns away into his singularity in 1976 itself, the twenty-first
of June thereof. In the light the room reasserts its smell of stale
smoke and perfumed disinfectant. It is a little before three o'clock.

In Port William now it is a little before six. Daylight, he imagines,
is reddening the sky over the wooded slopes of the little valley of
Harford Run, which falls away northward from his house; the treetops are misty in the damp morning air, a few stars and the waning
moon still bright in the sky. And he would be going out, if he were
there, with the milk bucket on his arm, calling the cows. Flora
would be starting breakfast, the children putting on their shoes,
half asleep, getting ready to go out to their own chores.

He is outside that, the air and light of that place filling his absence, the disturbance of his departure subsided. He looks back on
it as from somewhere far off in the sky. In the quieted place where
yesterday he went out, the children are now going out to do the
work that he went out to do, Flora going with them, probably, to
help them. He knows that she is being cheerful with them. Even if
she does not feel cheerful, she will be cheerful. She will be looking
for reasons to be cheerful, showing the children the slender moon
high up over the colored clouds of the dawn. She is saying, "Look,
Virgie, how the mist is hanging in the trees."

He would not have that grace himself. If he were going out into the morning aggrieved, he would be the embodiment of his grievance, and the day could be as bright as it pleased, yet it could not prevail upon him to be cheerful.

His right hand had been the one with which he reached out to the world and attached himself to it. When he lost his hand he lost his hold. It was as though his hand still clutched all that was dear to him—and was gone. All the world then became to him a steep slope, and he a man descending, staggering and falling, unable to reach out to tree trunk or branch or root to catch and hold on.

When he did reach out with his clumsy, hesitant, uneducated left hand, he would be maddened by its ineptitude. It went out as if fearful that it would displease him, and it did displease him. As he watched it groping at his buttons or trying to drive a nail or fumbling by itself with one of the two-handed tools that he now hated to use but would not give up, he could have torn it off and beaten it on the ground.

He remembered with longing the events of his body's wholeness, grieving over them, as Adam remembered Paradise. He remembered how his body had dressed itself, while his mind thought of something else; how he had shifted burdens from hand to hand; how his right hand had danced with its awkward partner and made it graceful; how his right hand had been as deft and nervous as a bird. He remembered his poise as a two-handed lover, when he reached out to Flora and held and touched her, until the smooths and swells of her ached in his palm and fingers, and his hand knew her as a man knows his homeland. Now the hand that joined him to her had been cast away, and he mourned over it as over a priceless map or manual forever lost.

One day Flora came to where he was sitting in the barn and he was crying. She put her arm around him. "It's going to be all right."

And he said, "What did they do with my hand?" For it had occurred to him that he did not know what they had done with it. Had
they burned it or buried it or just indifferently thrown it away?—
when they should have given it back to him to bring home and lay
properly to rest.

"What?" Flora said.

"What did they do with my hand? The goddamned sons of
bitches!"

Flora took her arm away. "*What* is the *matter* with you?"

"Just leave me alone."

Alone was the way she left him. Alone was the way he was, as cast
away there in his place as his hand was, wherever it was.

It is three o'clock. It is a little after three. He thinks of the lighted,
night-filled, shadowy streets. He has no purpose at all. There is now
simply nothing in the world that he intends. He looks at the opened,
rumpled bed. He intends at least not to go back there. He would as
soon lie down in his grave as in that bed.

He goes to the window, parts the heavy curtains, and looks down
into the empty street that seems to sleep and dream in the undis-
turbed fall of its shadows and weak lights. And he could be anybody
in the world awake in the night, looking out. "How much longer?"
he thinks. "When shall I arise, and the night be gone?"

They passed the winter alone, he and Flora, alone to each other, he
alone to all others. He lay awake to no purpose, as he would have
slept to no purpose, angry, sore, and baffled, willing to die if he
could have died, tossing to and fro unto the dawning of the day.
That he was alone was his own fault, he knew. He was wrong. And
yet he could not escape the fault and the wrong. He clutched them
to himself as he was clutched by them. He made no difference.

Nor did he work to any purpose, it seemed to him, except survival and the slow coming of dexterity to his left hand. The hand learned with the slowness of a tree growing, as if it had time and patience that he did not have.

And he was learning just as slowly to use the mechanical hook that he now wore on the stump of his right forearm, a stiff, frictionless, feelingless claw that would do some of the things he needed done and would not do others. It fitted his arm clumsily and fitted his work clumsily. The only thing pertaining to it that was fitting was the curse upon it that was shaped and ready in his mouth the moment he put it on.

He now had a left hand and something less good than a left hand, less good than a shod foot: an awkward primitive claw. And the two, the poor hand and the poor claw, did not cooperate, meeting together in the air, dancing together, as his two hands had done, but for the simplest task required all of his mind, all of his deliberation and will, so that he wearied of them and cursed them. There was the problem of balance. He repeatedly set and braced himself, addressing his right hand to some task, only to discover again that the hand was gone.

He continued by the help of time alone. He went on, not because he would not have stopped, but because nothing else would stop. Through the winter he tended to his animals and kept the little farm alive. Flora helped him and so did the children, watchful of him, always apprehensive of his anger, but giving him patience and kindness that he knew he had not earned and did not repay. He knew that Flora talked to the children about him. He knew, as well as if he had overheard, what she had said. "Well, now, listen. This is a hard time for your daddy. You'll have to understand and be patient with him. He'll be better after while." This was what she said to the children, he knew, because it was what she said to herself. And he could see them watching him, Virgie and Betty, as if for confirmation of what she had told them. That he was a trouble to them he knew, and regretted, and the knowledge only deepened his anger at himself and turned him harder against them.

At the edge of his anger at everything else was always his anger at himself. He was ashamed of himself. He had betrayed his hand. He had put his precious hand into a machine that had obliged him by continuing to do what he had started it doing, as if he had not changed his mind. His hand had been given to him for a helpmeet, to love and to cherish, until he died, and he had been unfaithful to it. He was guilty and he was angry at himself. And yet he turned away. The place of his guilt and shame was like the unknown ocean of the early maps, full of monsters. He knew it was there, but he did not go there.

He could not yet drive a team. He did not trust himself to try that, and for good reason: His left hand had not yet come up to the job; it was strong enough, but not discriminating enough; it had not yet taken responsibility for being the only hand he had. His son, Virgil, could drive the team, was good at it for a boy, but Virgie was only twelve years old. He wanted to do more, and undoubtedly was capable of doing more, than Andy would allow him to do. For Andy was afraid. Catastrophe lived at the end of his arm. Whatever Virgie did, Andy could see how he could be hurt or killed, how the world might simply shrug him off, as a big horse would shrug off a fly. And so Virgie did not do the jobs with the team that he would have had to do alone, but only those at which Andy could be with him, ready to instruct or caution or help.

"We add up to pretty near a man," he said to Virgie, and Virgie gave him a look.

"No," Andy said. "You're pretty near a man yourself."

He was moved by Virgie, who was so able a boy and so willing to help, whatever it cost him, and often it cost him a great deal. The words of Andy's bitterness were always prepared; he uttered them before he thought them. Virgie did the best he could, and he did well, and yet in moments of stress or difficulty Andy imposed a demand that it seemed to him he did not even will: He wanted the boy to be as answerable to his thought as his right hand had been. He wanted the boy to *be* his right hand.

"*Come* on, Virgie!" he would say. "Come on! Come on!"

Or he would say, "*No*, damn it! Hit it *there*!"

Virgie, half crying with indignation, would say, "I'm *trying*, Dad!"

And Andy would say, "Try *harder*."

He was wrong, and knew it. He yearned toward the boy. His anger revealed his love, and yet removed him from it. He seemed to himself far away from all that he loved, too far away to help or to be helped. The pain he gave to Virgie, he saw, stood between him and Flora, and was his shame, and could not be helped. There were days when he could not bear the eyes of his daughter Betty, who saw everything, and loved him, and was hurt by him, and could not be helped.

"Daddy," she said, "are you all right?" And then, correcting herself, "Are you going to be all right?"

"Sure," he said.

He went as an exile into his own house and barn and fields. His wound had showed him the world and, at the same time, his estrangement from it. It was as though he continued to speak to his hand, which did not answer. And this was a loss of speech that could not be spoken of to anyone still whole and alive.

He felt his father watching him, worried about him, and he shied away.

His mother gave him no chance to shy away. "Come sit here," she said, reminding him for the first time of her mother.

"Andy, I'm sorry for what's happened. I can't tell you how sorry. But you must learn something from it."

"Learn!"

"What you don't know, you'll have to learn."

"What?"

"I don't know. But you must accept this as given to you to learn from, or it will hurt you worse than it already has."

He knew that she had missed nothing. He sat under her words with his head down as he had sat, when he was a boy, under a scolding. But she was not scolding.

"Given!" he said.

"You haven't listened," she said, reminding him again of his grandmother. "But don't forget."

He had become a special case, and he knew what he thought of that. He raged, and he raged at his rage, and nothing that he had was what he wanted. He remained devoted to his lost hand, to his body as it had been, to his life as he had wanted it to be; he could not give them up. That he had lost them and they were gone did not persuade him. The fact had no power with him. The powerlessness of the fact made him lonely, and he held to his loneliness to protect his absurdity. But it was as though his soul had withdrawn from his life, refusing any longer to live in it.

He was out of control. He *is* out of control. For months now he has not had the use of his best reasons. He is where he is, two thousand miles from home, where nobody knows where he is, in a room he has never seen before, because of a schedule that he made once and did not especially want to make when he made it. For months he has merely fallen from one day to another, with no more intention than any other creature or object that is falling, only seeing afterwards, too late, what his intention might have been, but by then fallen farther.

And this fall of his involved or revealed or caused the fall of appearances. He no longer trusted the look or sound of anything. He no longer believed that anything was what it appeared to be. He began to ask what had been secretly meant or ignorantly meant or unconsciously meant. And once his trust had failed there was no limit to his distrust; he saw that the world of his distrust was bottomless and forever dark, it was his fall itself, but he could not stop it.

He had long known that his quarrels with Flora proceeded along a line of complaints that they were, in fact, not about—or this had been true of their quarrels in the old days, before he had given his hand to the machine. Then their quarrels, as he knew or would know sooner or later in the course of them, were about duality: they were two longing to be one, or one dividing relentlessly into two. Their marriage seemed to live according to no logic at all, or none that he could see. It was the origin of the quarrel that divided them, and the selfsame quarrel, having consumed whatever fuel occasion may have offered it, would join them together again, and they met in an ease and joy that Andy knew they did not make, and that he at least did not deserve. It was as though grace and peace were bestowed on them out of the sanctity of marriage itself, which simply furnished them to one another, free and sufficient as rain to leaf. It was as if they were not making marriage but being made by it, and, while it held them, time and their lives flowed over them, like swift water over stones, rubbing them together, grinding off their edges, making them fit together, fit to be together, in the only way that fragments can be rejoined. And though Andy did not understand this, and though he suffered from it, he trusted it and rejoiced in it.

And then his trust failed, because his trust in himself failed. He had no faith in himself, and he had no faith in her faith in him, or in his faith in her. Now their quarrels did not end their difference and bring them together, but were all one quarrel that had no end. It changed subjects, but it did not end. It was no longer about duality, but about division, an infinite cold space that opened between them. It fascinated him and held him, even as he feared and hated it. Always there was something that he burned to say about it.

At times, in their quarreling, he knew he was crying out to her across that abyss, and he knew she heard him but would not pretend it was a call she could answer. Sometimes he knew he was crying for her to pity him for his dissatisfaction with her. He knew there was no door leading out from that. If he wanted to be free of it, he must stop it himself, and receive no congratulation from her for stopping it. He knew he was living the life history of a fraction, and that the fraction was growing smaller. He saw no help for it.

"Do you know what you need?" she said to him one day.

"What?"

"Forgiveness. And I want to forgive you. All of us do. And you need more than ours. But you must forgive yourself."

She was crying, and he pitied her. And he knew she had told the truth, and it made him furious.

He did not trust her to love him. He did not trust himself to trust her to love him.

"You don't love me."

He made her furious, and was glad of it, and was sorry he was glad.

He could not win his quarrel with her and he could not quit it.

Nothing in his life had ever so exhausted him. He would sit in the kitchen at night, after the children were asleep, and argue with her. All his effort would be to keep his anger and his distrust, the real subjects of the quarrel, in the dark or in disguise.

She would meet his attacks bravely, hopelessly, often in tears. "It's *you* you're talking about. It's not me. You're mad at me because I can't stop you from being mad at yourself."

He would change the line of his attack, returning to his little trove of complaints against her, and she would check him.

"That's true. But it's not what you mean. You don't trust me. Or yourself. You have no faith."

She was right, and he could not win. But he knew nevertheless how to wound her. He would perform another flanking movement and attack again. He was ingenious. He was never at a loss. The agility of his maneuvers surprised him, and he took a mean pleasure in them. He persisted toward a cessation and a peace that he could not achieve. And finally he mystified himself. At some point in the quarrel he would realize that he could not remember how it had started or how it had proceeded or what it was about, that he was lost in its mere presence, as beginningless and endless as a nightmare. And through it all he felt inside him the small, hard knot of his guilt.

Only exhaustion stopped him. Finally, worn and emptied by his hopeless anger and Flora's hopeless resistance, he would have barely the strength to walk to bed. In bed, her back turned to him, he would lie awake. And then he would sleep, but only to dream a dream that would wake him and keep him awake in fear.

He dreamed that it became necessary to set fire to his house, and he set it afire, only to realize, as the flames altogether enveloped it, that his family was inside.

He dreamed that he was in a battle, about to throw a hand grenade. He hesitated, thinking of the humanity of those he meant to destroy, and the grenade exploded in his hand.

He was walking up the creek road. A woman with snaky hair was standing on the roadside, looking down at the water. He meant to pass by her and not be seen. As he drew even with her, she turned and with her stony eyes looked him full in the face. At his outcry the room returned.

"What?" Flora said.

"Nothing."

He heard a heavy engine approaching. He ran around the house and stood beside Flora. A spotlight, surprisingly near, shone directly on them. He cried out, "*Hey!*" and woke.

He picks up the hook where he left it on the floor, too strange to belong anywhere, incomplete in itself, helpless to complete any other thing, and begins putting it on. His hand fumbles at the fastenings. He labors under the balking impulse to use his right hand to install the hook on his right arm. Finally he is taken again by rage at the oddity of his handless arm and the hook and his incompetent left hand. He flings the hook into the waste basket, pleased by the sound of the heavy fall of it. "Lie there where you belong, you rattledy bastard!"

He goes into the bathroom and without turning on the light fills the basin with cold water and lifts it to his face, handful after handful, grateful for the coldness and wetness of it, and dries his face and hand. He feels in his shaving kit for his comb and combs his hair, and stands still again in the twilit little cubicle, waiting for a new intention to move him.

He is coming near to the end of a long labor of self-exhaustion. He is almost empty now. The world is almost absent from him. It is as though he still stands, emptied and shaking, behind the rostrum in his last moments at the conference. The conference was about, and was meant to promote, the abstractions by which things and lives are transformed into money. It was meant, as if by some voiceless will within the speaking voices, to seize upon actual lives and cause them to disappear into something such as the Future of the American Food System. He is oppressed by all that has oppressed him for months, but now also by the memory of his voice and of all the other voices at the conference, abstraction welling up into them, a great black cloud of forgetfulness. Soon they would not remember who or where they were, their dear homeland drawn up into the Future of the American Food System to be seen no more, forever destroyed by schemes, by numbers, by deadly means, all its springs poisoned. For years Andy has been moved by the possibility of acting in opposition to this, but he does not feel it now. It has gone away. He feels himself strangely fixed, cut off, unable to want either to stand or to move.

And yet there is a memory flickering in the stump of his arm, and it is not that of the clasp of the hooks' fastenings. It is the imprint of the thumb and fingers of a man's hand, hard, forthright, and friendly.

When his first crop of alfalfa was ready to harvest in mid May, they came to help him—Nathan and Danny and Jack, and Martin and Arthur Rowanberry. Or, rather, they came and harvested his hay, he helping them, and doing it poorly enough in his own opinion, with embarrassment, half resenting their charitable presumption, embarrassing them by his self-apology.

Nathan, who ran the crew—because Andy was useless to do it, and somebody had to do it—mainly ignored him, except to give him orders in the form of polite questions: "Don't you think it'll do to go up this afternoon?" "What about you running the rake?"

When they were finished, Andy, speaking as he knew out of the worst of his character, said, "I don't know how to thank you. I don't know how I can ever repay you."

And speaking out of the best of his, Nathan said, "Help *us*." So saying, he looked straight at Andy, grinned, took hold of his right forearm, and gave just a little tug.

That was in another world. That memory in the flesh of his arm could not be stranger if it were some spirit's parting touch that he had borne with him into the womb.

The incident gave him no ease. It placed an expectation on him that he could not refuse and did not want. He did go to help them, but only as a nuisance, he felt, to them and to himself. He had little belief that they needed him or that he could help them. And, faced with his uncertainty, they seemed not to know what to ask of him. Except, that is, for Nathan. Nathan ignored him as he was, and treated him as if he were a stranger who required an extraordinary nicety of manners, speaking to him almost exclusively in polite questions. How would he feel about doing this? Would he mind too much doing that?

And all of this was characteristic of Nathan, who had known a war that was his country's and his time's, and who had made a peace that was his own. He entirely lacked the strenuous dissatisfactions with self and circumstance and other people that had been so much a part of the bond between Andy and Elton. He was Andy's third cousin on Andy's father's side, and he was, in a fashion, the son-in-law of Andy's mother's father, Mat Feltner. He was a good, quiet man, as if he were Mat's blood son as well as the husband of his onetime daughter-in-law. There was an accuracy of generosity in Nathan that Andy wondered at, and no nonsense. He said little and spoke well. And Andy began to live in a kind of fear of him. That clamp of Nathan's hand, by which Nathan had meant to in-

clude him, excluded him. Because he could not answer it, it lived
upon his flesh like a burn, the brand of his exile.

As though Nathan is standing beside him now in the little dark
room, Andy turns away. He begins to dress, avoiding the mirror
now, fearfully, as if, looking in, he might see himself with the head
of a toad. He does not think, but only feels. He does not think of the
origin of the pain he feels, or of the anger hollow and dry in his heart.

And now, dressing, he hurries to get out. He has begun to hear
again the night noises of the city. He has known the city since his
first travels, nearly twenty years ago, and he feels it around him
now, standing stepped and graceful on its heights, and around it the
always arriving sea, the sea and the sky reaching westward, past the
land's edge, out of sight.

He darkens the room and goes out into the dim hallway and the
interior quiet of the building, away from the street sounds. The long
hall is carpeted, and he goes silently past the shut doors of rooms
where people are sleeping or absent, who would know which?
There is an almost palpable unwaking around him as he goes past
the blank doors, intent upon his own silence, as though, his presence known to nobody, he is not there himself.

At the elevator he stops and looks at the button saying "Down."
But he does not push it. He does not want to hear the jolt of machinery as the elevator begins to rise, or the long groan of its rising,
or the jolt of its stopping, the doors clanking open. He does not
want to enter that little box and see it close upon him and be carried
passively downward in it.

He goes on along the corridor and lets himself out into the stair-
well. He has made no noise, but now his steps echo around him as
he descends the rightward turning stairs, five floors, to the lobby,
where the carpet silences them again.

The lobby is deserted. The empty chairs sit in conversational groups of two and three, their cushions dented. There is no one behind the desk. The clock over the desk says twenty after four.

What have I done with the time?

Remembering as if far back, he knows what he did with it. He stood up there in the room like a graven image of himself, telling over the catalogue of his complaints. There is a country inside him where his complaints live and do their work, where they invite him to come, offering their enticements and tidbits, the self-justifications of anger, the self-justifications of self-humiliation, the coddled griefs.

When he looks at the clock again, it is almost four-thirty. *This is happening to my soul. This is a part of the life history of my soul.* Outside in the street a car passes, stops for the light at the corner, its engine idling, and then turns and goes on. He must go. He must get outside. He is filled suddenly with panic, as though the doors have begun to grow rapidly smaller.

3.

Remembering

In the street the wind comes fresh against him, smelling a little of the sea. He stands outside the hotel entrance, the street all his own for the moment. Off in the distance he can hear a siren baying, and then another joining it. A taxi eases up to the intersection nearby, waits for the light, and eases on. Two or three blocks away a garbage compressor utters a loud yawn followed by something like a swallow. And underneath the noises there is a silence as of the sleep of almost everybody, and beside or within the silence a low mechanical hum.

A frail-looking woman passes by, drunk and walking unsteadily but with an attempt anyway at dignity, holding her jacket closed at the throat as if she is cold. Watching her, he feels his silence. An unknown world would have to be crossed for him to speak to her. And yet something in him for which he has no word cries out toward her, for the world between them fails in their silence, who are alone and heavy laden and without rest. *This is the history of souls. This is the earthly history of immortal souls.*

He begins to walk slowly past the deserted entries, the darkened windows. A truck passes, shifting into a lower gear as the grade steepens. Somewhere there is an outcry, a man's voice, distressed and urgent, unintelligible. A car engine starts. The garbage truck again raises its wail.

Other night walkers appear, meet him and pass and go on, or go by on the cross streets. They are far between, alone. He can hear their steps, each one, echoing in the spaces around him. It is the time of night, he thinks, when the dying die— *O greens, and fields, and trees, farewell, farewell!*—and the dead lie stillest in their graves, when the dying who are not yet to die begin again to live.

A man overtakes and passes him, carrying a lunch box, walking fast. He meets a woman with long blonde hair, dressed in leotards, spike heels, and a zebra-striped cloth coat. He sees a couple crossing an intersection ahead of him, young and beautiful, their arms around each other, going home. He imagines them risen from their fallen clothes like resurrected souls, stepping toward one another open-armed.

The city at night, he thinks, is like the forest at night, when most creatures have no need to stay awake, but some do, and that is well, for the place itself must never sleep. Some must carry wakefulness through the sleep of others.

He is walking northward, along Mason, toward Aquatic Park. He wants to reach the city's edge. He longs for the verge and immensity of the continent's meeting with the sea. Stopping now and then to listen and to turn and look down into the street behind him, he climbs slowly up the steepening hill. It is shadowy and dim between the street lights; above him, above the building tops, the sky is dark, its still spaces measured out by stars and the dwindling moon. He pauses by a tiny garden behind a wall, dusky and still amid the buildings; it contains a few dark shrubs and flowers whose pale blossoms seem to float in the shadows. A bird is singing there, and another somewhere toward the top of the hill. The dawn must be beginning now; there must be a little paling in the eastern sky, invisible yet within the city's bright horizon. But at the next cross street, looking eastward across the bay, he sees a cloud with just the first suggestion of daylight touching its underside.

At the top of the hill the Fairmont is brightly lighted. The pavement in front has just been washed, and the lights shine in the wet. Andy stops on the corner to look. He would like to go into the lobby and see it, opulent and empty so early in the morning. He almost does so, and then stops, remembering himself: a one-handed man, unshaven and carelessly dressed. He does not want some elegant-mannered doorman or clerk to ask him, "May I *help* you?" He stands and looks and goes by, and on across the hilltop and onto the downward slant of the street. Behind him a robin is singing in the foliage of one of the cropped sycamores in front of the Pacific Union, and he can hear a street sweeper whistling prettily over the harsh strokes of his broom.

There are trees now, here and there along the street, their crowns dark. As he passes under one of them a bird begins to sing in it, a complex lyric sung as if forgotten all through the night and now remembered. Now wherever trees are, singing is in them. Where the buildings are the city is, and is quiet. Where the trees are the world is, and a sweet worldsong is singing itself in the dark.

He is a walker in the dark, excluded from the songs around him.

Taxis are creeping along the empty streets almost silently, like beasts of prey. A baby cries, and high in a dark wall to his left a window is suddenly lighted. At the corner of Jackson Street he stops while a noisy Volkswagen bus pauses at the intersection, but when the bus shifts gears and goes on, Andy continues to stand still, looking down Jackson at the bay. He can see the lights of the Bay Bridge stepping out into the air above the dark water. He can hear the cable car cable humming under the street. A man in a hooded shirt, walking a dog, crosses Jackson and goes on up the hill, his steps echoing in the quiet. Andy is filled with a yearning toward this place. He imagines himself living here. He would have a small apartment up here on the hillside, a cliff dwelling, looking out over the bay. He would live alone, and slowly he would come to know a peacefulness and gentleness in his own character, having nobody to quarrel with. He would have a job that he could walk to in the morning and walk home from in the evening. It would be a job that would pay him well and give him nothing to worry about before he went to it or after he left it. In his spare time he would visit the museums. He would dress well and eat well. He would learn Japanese and spend his vacations in Japan. He would become a student of Japanese culture and art. He would bring back pottery and paintings. His apartment would be a place of refuge, quiet and orderly, full of beautiful things. In his travels he would meet beautiful, indolent, slow-speaking women as solitary and independent as himself, who would not wish to know him well.

But he reminds himself of himself. Something else in him is raging at him: "Damn you! Damn you!" And he says then lucidly to his mind, "Yes, you sorry fool, be still!" For the flaw in all that dream is himself, the little hell of himself alone.

You fool. You sorry fool.

The cable hums under the street. The bridge swings its great stride out into the dark. Now the city parcels itself out in his hearing: the hum of the cable almost underfoot, and in the distance the hum of the night-waking of the whole city. Except for those sounds near and far, for the moment it is quiet, and he can hear the birds singing wherever there are trees. The birds brood or dream over their song, as if the song knows of the coming light that the birds have not yet suspected. The time is neither night nor morning.

He reminds himself of himself.

He walks again, crossing on Jackson to Powell, and turning again northward. The names on windows and awnings are in Chinese now. The street reeks with the smell of yesterday's fish.

A figure lurches upright out of a doorway ahead of him. The man is bearded, long-haired, his head bound with a rolled bandanna. He wears a fringed buckskin coat.

"Hey, man!"

"Hello!"

"Say, brother, could you spare me a buck for a little breakfast?"

Andy feels in his pocket, finding, if he is not mistaken, two nickels and a quarter. "I thought the toll was a dime."

"This ain't 1930, man."

"Well, when is it?"

"How would *I* know? Later?"

Am I going to show this fellow my wallet?

Holding his wallet in his one hand, he will be disarmed.

"I mean, a good breakfast, man, that's a good start on a good day." The man is chanting, dancing a little, as if to a rhythm independent of himself that might carry him abruptly up the street, empty-handed.

Do I even have a dollar bill? Is this charity or madness?

Madness or charity, he holds his wallet against his waist with his right forearm, and with his left hand plucks out a bill, and it is a five, and another, and it is a one; on impulse, he gives them both.

"Oh, wow! Far out! Thanks, Tex. You a man of a better time."

So would I hope, if I hoped, to pray to be.

When he has crossed Broadway he can see the lights of the westward tower of the Bay Bridge centered in the opening of the street, the lights of its cables swaying down symmetrically on either side. Above a dark cloudbank in the east, a pale light is in the sky. The traffic along Broadway is thin but constant, its sound established, the day begun.

A walker in the dark, he feels the touch of the light of the sky around him, but he is not in it. He reminds himself of himself.

In Washington Square, the trees are loud with the cries of sparrows. The little park is an island, green, tree-shaded under the lights; on the far side is the lighted pale front of the church of Peter and Paul. Andy sits down on a bench in the shadows near the firemen's monument. The sparrows clamor overhead. Lighted buses go by, the people inside them sleepy and quiet, on their way to work; as the buses move and stop, the people sway in unison in their seats, unresisting as underwater weeds. Joggers pass, striding long, their breathing loud over their footfalls. A dog passes slowly, his short legs trotting fast. A fat Chinese woman walks by, swinging her arms vigorously. Behind her comes a Chinese man slowly rotating his extended arms as if he is a sluggish seabird preparing to fly.

Now Andy can see daylight in all the sky, brighter to the east, although, below, the lights of the streets are still strong and the shadows dark. He sits and watches. He watches the slow waking of the streets, the gentle people exercising in the park, their movements as fluent and quiet as if dreamed. He watches the lights around the square become weak as the sky brightens. On the bench next to him a man is lying asleep under a blanket. In all the stirring in the square, they two are the only ones who are still. When the daylight has come well into the shadows and the night has entirely gone, he gets up; he stands in front of the church and reads the legend engraved across its face: LA GLORIA DI COLUI CHE TUTTO MUOVE PER L'UNIVERSO PENETRA E RISPLENDE.

GOOD EARTH REALTY, INC., and all the rest of the businesses along Columbus Avenue are still shut, dreaming perhaps of opportunities to come later. In their dreams their mouths are open, and people are rushing in with their pockets full of money. There is nothing like a crowd yet in the gray light of the street. The walkers, some going to work, some going to breakfast, some led by little dogs, appear one at a time, widely dispersed, moved along by singular and undetectable purposes.

What draws him to the sleeper in the doorway, he does not know. He sees the man lying there, his knees drawn up beneath a short piece of blanket that does not cover his feet, and he stops. He stops, perhaps, because of some suggestion of the power of his awareness over the man sleeping unaware. The man, Andy sees, is young, his face unlined under his three days' growth of beard. His hair is blond, his beard red. His head is resting on his extended right arm, the forearm propped at the wrist against the kick plate of the door, the hand relaxed and drooping like the bloom of a nodding flower. The hand, like the blanket, is dirty. The young man's mouth is slightly open. He has the innocent look of a sleeping child. And what can have brought him here?

Andy leans, looking at the young man face to face. The young man is loosened and easy in his sleep, in his vulnerability unaware, as if in some absolute trust that to Andy is not imaginable. The sleeper has entrusted himself to his defenseless sleep as confidently as a little child to his own bed at home. As if not with his mind but with his shoulder and breastbone, Andy recalls his grandfather's old fingers prodding him through the covers. "Boy? The sun's up." And then, in pity and sorrow: "And you still a-laying in the bed with the daylight in your face." And Andy thinks of himself leaning over his own sleeping son. For a moment he is almost breathless with the thought that if he reached out and touched this man, he would move; he would stir and wake out of his dark sleep to live in this new day that has come.

But now singing is in the street, and Andy moves away. A man is coming up the street, singing an aria in a fine, strong tenor. As he moves along he is inspecting the interiors of garbage cans, as unfailing in his attentions as a postman. As they meet and pass, the man does not look at Andy. He seems to be aware of nothing in the world but his quest from garbage can to garbage can. He seems not to hear himself singing.

"No," Andy thinks. "Maybe it was not absolute trust. Maybe it was absolute despair. Maybe when he lay down he didn't care if he slept or died." Andy lays his hand on his breastbone as a chill or an ache passes through him and shakes him. He reminds himself of himself.

He is down in the flat now, close to the bay. At intersections he can see Alcatraz with its walls, its lighthouse flashing. A nice gentle-faced woman is waiting at a bus stop alone. Andy says before he thinks, as if in Port William, "Morning!" The woman quickly looks away. Her fear and accusation are in the air around her, leaving him hardly room to pass.

But momentum is going with him now. He is almost outside the network of the streets. And then, at the foot of Hyde Street, he *is* out of it and is standing in the great fall of dawnlight over the bay and its islands, the Golden Gate, the Marin hills and Mount Tamalpais beyond. To the east, beyond the Berkeley hills, the whiteness of the sky has begun to show a faint stain of pink. The air opens and lightens around him, freshening, bearing the cold pungence of the ocean. Seagulls, crying hungrily, circle on spread wings in the unobstructed day.

In Aquatic Park a little lilting surf is running up the beach, the tide going out, and gulls are walking with strange terrestrial flatfootedness among the windrows of drift and trash and seaweed. Andy goes along the curved walk above the harbor into the lee of the high ground of Fort Mason where the air is still and he can smell the eucalyptus trees.

The long pier curves out ahead of him into the bay. He is going over water now. A few fishermen are already leaning on the parapet, watching their lines, which disappear beneath the little waves. The fishermen are already dazzled with expectation and the motion of the water. As Andy stands and watches, a rod tip suddenly vibrates and gestures downward.

A little farther out he encounters suddenly the wind off the sea, pressing in massively and steadily past the bridge. The gulls go against it, and turn, their wings spread to it in overmastering grace; their voices skitter and quarrel over tidbits of garbage or the possible future occurrence of tidbits of garbage. Out toward Alcatraz seven pelicans are flying in stately single file. Westward, the great bridge stands aloof, its tower tops hidden in fog, and out beyond it the immense tremor of the ocean. Fishing boats are coming in from the night. Gulls standing on the parapets of the pier call softly, and then for no apparent reason break into laughter.

Andy walks and stands and walks until he comes to the outermost arc of the pier. There, with the whole continent at his back, nothing between him and Asia but water, he stands again, leaning on the parapet, looking westward into the wind. The air has cleared beyond the bridge now; he can see ships there, waiting to come in; a tug is on its way out to meet one of them.

And now almost at Andy's feet, silently and with no disturbance at all, a head appears among the waves. One moment it was not there, and the next it is. It is a head so black and slick that Andy at first thinks it is the head of a man wearing a bathing cap. But it is the head of a sea lion who looks around with the intelligent gaze of a man, and then is gone so quickly and with so little disturbance that Andy, who was looking at it, cannot be sure when it went. So sudden, brief, and silent was its appearance, so intelligent its glossy eye, so perfect its absence, that when it rises again, Andy thinks, it may rise into a day two hundred years ago.

A gray freighter comes into sight, going out. So far away as it is, it is silent, moving steadily along, already submitted to the long pulse of its engines that will drive it out under the bridge, past the headlands, into the wild ocean. Going where?

Where might he not go? Who knows where he is? He feels the simplicity and lightness of his solitude. Other lives, other possible lives swarm around him.

Distance comes upon him. Nobody in thousands of miles, nobody who knows him, knows where he is. If Flora wanted him now, how would she find him? How would a call or letter find him with news of any death or grief? All distance is around him, and he wants nothing that he has. All choice is around him, and he knows nothing that he wants.

I've come to another of thy limits, Lord. Is this the end?

Out of the depths have I cried unto thee, O Lord.

Though he did not think of her, the words come to him in his grandmother's voice. They breathe themselves out of him in her voice and leave him empty, empty as if of his very soul. As though some corrosive light has flashed around him, he stands naked to time and distance, empty, and he has no thought.

He hears the sound of hoofbeats approaching on a gravel road. It is dusk. He sees a little boy standing barefoot on the stones of a driveway leading up to the paintless walls of an old house, about which the air seems tense with the memory of loss and dying not long past, of weeping and gnashing of teeth. The swifts, oblivious, circle in long sweeps over the roof of the house and hover over its chimneys. The boy watches the swifts, thinking of the sounds of rifle fire and of cannon, of the running of many horses, and of the dead sons of the house, so much older than he, so long gone, that he will think of them always as his father's sons, not as his brothers. He hears the nearer hoofbeats too, and he waits.

They turn in at the gate; he turns to look now, and sees that it is a good high-headed bay horse. The man riding the horse is square-built and has a large beard. The boy likes the man's eyes because they look straight at him and do not change and do not look away. The man stops beside the boy and crosses his hands over the pommel of the saddle.

"My boy, might your sister be home?"

"She ain't ever anyplace else, hardly."

"I see." The man thinks while he talks, and before, and after. "Well, can you show me where to put my horse?"

"Yessir."

"Do you want to ride?"

"Yessir." He does want to ride, for he loves the horse, and perhaps the man too.

The man reaches down with his hand. "Well, take a hold and give a jump."

The boy does as he is told, and is swung up behind the saddle.

"I'm Ben Feltner. Who are you?"

"Jack Beechum."

"That's what I thought."

Ben Feltner clucks to the horse.

"You came to see my sister?"

"Your sister is Nancy Beechum?"

"Yessir."

"Well, I came to see her."

That would have been 1868, and then and thus was the shuttle flung, for the first time in Andy's knowledge, through the web of his making. Beyond that meeting, Mat, his grandfather, wakens, crying, in his cradle, and Bess, Andy's mother, in hers, and Andy in his, and Andy's own children in theirs: Betty, named Elizabeth for his mother, and Virgie, named Virgil for his mother's brother, missing in action, presumed dead, in the Pacific in 1945.

Though the light is still gray on the pier and over the water, a few windows are shining on the hill above Sausalito. Weak sunlight, while Andy watches, begins to color the slopes of other hills north of the bridge, whitening the drifts of fog that lie in their hollows.

A gull is walking on the parapet nearby, crying loudly, "Ahhh! Ahhh!" It comes so close that Andy can see its bright eye and the clear bead of seawater quivering on its beak.

"What?" Andy says.

The gull says, "Ahhh!"

A sailboat passes, its sail unraised, its engine running slowly and quietly. The tug has met its ship and they are starting in.

Again hoofbeats approach him over gravel, and he sees an old man coming on horseback through the same gate through the mist and slow rain of a morning in early March. Except for the strength of the light, the warming air, and a certain confidence in the surrounding birdsong, it still looks like the dead of winter. The pastures are brown, the trees bare. The house, though, is painted, and the whole place, which in 1868 looked almost forgotten, has obviously been remembered again and for a long time kept carefully in mind. It is seventy-seven years later. The old man on the horse is a little past seventy-five. He wears neatly a canvas hunting coat frayed at the cuffs and a felt hat creased in the crown by long wear and darkened by the rain. The horse is a rangy sorrel gelding, who, by the look of his eye, requires a master, which, by his gait and deportment, is what he has on his back. As he rides, the old man is looking around.

He goes up beside the house and through the gate into the barn lot and into the barn.

"Whoa," he says. "Hello."

"Hello," a voice says from the hayloft.

There are footsteps on the loft floor and then a scrape, and a large forkful of hay drops onto the barn floor.

The horse snorts and lunges backward. The old man sits him straight up and unsurprised. "Whoa," he says, and with hand and heel forces the horse back up into the tracks he stood in before. With a little white showing in his eye, breathing loud, the horse stands in them, quivering. He does not offer to move again.

A young man comes down the loft ladder. "I'm sorry. I didn't hear your horse."

"It's all right."

The old man waits, and the young man comes up by the horse's left shoulder, laying a hand on his neck. "Whoa, boy."

"I'm Marce Catlett. I'm your neighbor. I've come to make your acquaintance."

The old man reaches down his hand and the young man reaches up and takes it.

"I'm Elton Penn, Mr. Catlett."

Each knows the other by reputation, and each looks for the marks of what he has heard.

The old man sees that the young man's clothes are old, well mended, and well worn. He sees that he has a straight, clear look in his eye. He sees the good team of horses standing in their stalls, and their harness properly hung up.

The young man sees the respect the sorrel horse has for his rider, and vice versa, the excellent fettle of the horse, the old saddle and bridle well attended, and he recognizes the exacting workman, the man of careful satisfactions whom he has heard about.

"I think you know Wheeler Catlett," Marce says. "He's my boy. He thinks a lot of you."

"Yessir. I think a lot of him."

Elton stands with his hand on the horse's neck. Marce sits looking over Elton's and the horse's heads into the barn.

"Well, Jack Beechum was my neighbor all my life."

He looks back down at Elton and considers and says, "Jack Beechum is a good man. He's been a good one. None better."

"That's what I hear." Elton says, "I haven't met Mr. Beechum yet."

"Well, when you do, you'll know him for what he is. You'll see it in him."

Now, as by agreement, they turn and look out across the lot at the house, Elton no longer touching the horse.

"I've got two grandboys. Wheeler's. They'll be over to bother you, I expect, now that the weather's changing. You won't offend me if you make 'em mind."

"Yessir."

Elton's wife, Mary, comes out the kitchen door with a dishpan of water, crosses the yard, and flings the dirty water over the pasture fence. She comes back, stepping in a hurry, waves to the two of them, smiles, and goes back into the kitchen. Marce has watched her attentively, going out and coming back, and out of the corner of his eye Elton has watched him watching.

"Son, you've got a good woman yonder. She'll cook a man a meal of vittles before you know it."

"Thank you, sir."

They are again silent a moment, and then Marce says, "Well, you'll do all right. Go ahead."

Without any signal from Marce that Elton sees or hears, the horse steps back into the swift, easy stride that brought him.

"Come back, Mr. Catlett."

"I will that."

"Old man Marce Catlett will neighbor with you, if you treat him right," Elton had been told before he moved. It proved true. Marce and Dorie Catlett and Elton and Mary Penn were neighbors, and in that neighborhood, Andy and Henry grew familiar and learned much.

It did not last long as it began. It was the end of something old and long that Andy was born barely in time to know. Old Jack Beechum was already gone from his place. In two years Marce was dead, the horse and mule teams were going, the tractors and other large machines were coming, the old ways were ending.

After Marce's death, Andy came to stay with his grandmother, to help her and to be company for her. He was a restless boy, and to keep him occupied, she gave him all the eggs that her dominicker hens laid outside the henhouse. After school, he searched out the hidden nests in the barns and outbuildings, and put the eggs a few at a time into a basket in a closet. Through that early spring of Marce's death, the grieved old woman and the eager boy talked of his project. He would save the eggs until he had enough, and then sell them, and with the money buy a setting of eggs of another kind from a neighbor. "Buff Orpingtons," Dorie said. "They're fine chickens. You can raise them to frying size and sell them, and then you'll have some money to put in the bank."

"And next year we'll raise some more."

"Maybe we will."

The evening comes when they put the eggs under a setting hen in the henhouse. He is holding the marked eggs in a basket, and Dorie is taking them out one by one and putting them under the hen.

"You know, you can just order the chickens from a factory now, and they send them to you through the mail."

"But this is the *best* way, ain't it?" He hopes it is, for he loves it.

"It's the cheapest. And the oldest. It's been done this way a long time."

"How long, do you reckon?"

"Oh, forever."

She puts the last egg under the hen, and strokes her back as she would have stroked a baby to sleep. Out the door he can see the red sky in the west. And he loves it there in the quiet with her, doing what has been done forever.

"I hope we always do it forever," he says.

She looks down at him, and smiles, and then suddenly pulls his head against her. "Oh, my boy, how far away will you be sometime, remembering this?"

The wind blows his tears back like the earpieces of a pair of spectacles. The bridge has begun to shine. He turns and sees that the sun has risen and is making a path toward him across the water.

He is held, though he does not hold. He is caught up again in the old pattern of entrances: of minds into minds, minds into place, places into minds. The pattern limits and complicates him, singling him out in his own flesh. Out of the multitude of possible lives that have surrounded and beckoned to him like a crowd around a star, he returns now to himself, a mere meteorite, scorched, small, and fallen. He has met again his one life and one death, and he takes them back. It is as though, leaving, he has met himself already returning, pushing in front of him a barn seventy-five feet by forty, and a hundred acres of land, six generations of his own history, partly failed, and a few dead and living whose love has claimed him forever. He will be partial, and he will die; he will live out the truth of that. Though he does not hold, he is held. He is grieving, and he is full of joy. What is that Egypt but his Promised Land?

Word of death and grief *has* reached him, and it is word of his own death and grief, which are his life too, his remembering and his joy.

"Boys," Mat says, "it was a *hot* day. There wasn't a breeze anywhere in that bottom that would have moved a cobweb. It was punishing." He is telling Elton and Andy.

It was a long time ago. Mat was only a boy yet, though he was nearly grown. His Uncle Jack hired him to help chop out a field of tall corn in a creek bottom. It was hot and still, and the heat stood close around them as they worked. They felt they needed to tiptoe to get enough air.

Mat thought he could not stand it any longer, and then he stood it a little longer, and they reached the end of the row.

"Let's go sink ourselves in the creek," Jack said.

They did. They hung their sweated clothes on willows in the sun to dry, and sank themselves in the cool stream up to their noses. It was a good hole, deep and shady, with the sound of the riffles above and below, and a kingfisher flying in and seeing them and flying away. All that afternoon when they got too hot, they went there.

"Well sir," Mat says, "it made that hard day good. I thought of all the times I'd worked in that field, hurrying to get through, to get to a better place, and it had been there all the time. I can't say I've always lived by what I learned that day—I wish I had—but I've never forgot."

"What?" Andy says.

"That it was there all the time."

"What?"

"Redemption," Mat says, and laughs. "A little flowing stream."

Beside Andy, the city stands on its hills, beyond the last dry pull across the rocks, the last dead mule and broken wheel. He can hear it, all its voices and engines washed together in the long murmur of its waking.

Once, years ago, he and Flora and their friend Hal Jimson stood on Tamalpais, all the world below them covered with fog, and heard that murmur, low and far away, as of a country remembered. The sea of fog, white to the horizons, gleamed below them, and, in the draws of the mountain, swallows swung and dived in their hunting flights as though they moved in the paths of some unutterable song.

And that was on the way. He is not going there.

All the Marin peninsula is in sunlight. So far away, so bright, it might be the shining land, the land beyond, which many travelers have seen, but never reached.

But the whole bay is shining now, the islands, the city on its hills, the wooden houses and the towers, the green treetops, the flashing waves and wings, the glory that moves all things resplendent everywhere.

4.

A Long Choosing

Though he has not moved, he has turned. *I must go now. If I am going to go, it is time.* On the verge of his journey, he is thinking about choice and chance, about the disappearance of chance into choice, though the choice be as blind as chance. That he is who he is and no one else is the result of a long choosing, chosen and chosen again. He thinks of the long dance of men and women behind him, most of whom he never knew, some he knew, two he yet knows, who, choosing one another, chose him. He thinks of the choices, too, by which he chose himself as he now is. How many choices, how much chance, how much error, how much hope have made that place and people that, in turn, made him? He does not know. He knows that some who might have left chose to stay, and that some who did leave chose to return, and he is one of them. Those choices have formed in time and place the pattern of a membership that chose him, yet left him free until he should choose it, which he did once, and now has done again.

Nancy Beechum had her father to keep house for and then nurse and then bury, and her brother to raise. Ben Feltner was her faithful and patient suitor for eleven years. They married in 1879, when she was thirty-four and he thirty-nine. They had five children, of whom Mat, after the perils of birth, accident, and epidemic, was the one survivor. Mat was the first Feltner in his own line to leave Port William after the first ones had come there at the beginning of the century, and by then it was the beginning of the next.

He did not go by his own choice. He went because he was sent; he was fifteen, and the time had come to send him, if he was going to go. He had been the subject of discussion between his father and his mother, he knew. And so he was discomforted but not surprised when one day, instead of leaving the dinner table when he was finished, his father remained in his place and thought, and looked at Nancy, and looked at Mat.

"Mat, my boy, we think highly of you, you know, and so we must part with you for a while."

They had arranged for him to attend a boarding school at Hargrave, run by a couple named Lowstudder. Mat did not want to go. He had never thought of going, and now that he had to think of it his reluctance took the shape of a girl, Margaret Finley, whom he had never not known, and whom, now that he thought of leaving her, he did not want to leave.

But when the time came he did leave her. Ben drove him to the landing and put him on the boat with a small trunk, and shook his hand and gripped his shoulder and said nothing and left him. They raised the gangplank, the little steamboat backed into the channel, and Mat watched the green water widen between him and his life as he knew it.

After three weeks Ben came to see him. Mat, summoned, found him sitting on the stile block where he had hitched his horse. He was smiling. He shook Mat's hand, and Mat sat down beside him.

"Do you like it here?"

"Nosir."

Ben, his hand flat on his beard, sat looking out at the big trees in the yard in front of them.

"Have you learned anything?"

"Yessir. Some."

Again Ben looked away and considered.

"Do you cry any of a night, son?"

"Nosir."

"Are you lonesome for Margaret Finley?"

"I miss you all too."

Ben stroked his hand slowly down his face and beard, thinking of something that made him smile.

"You're a good boy, Mat. I think you'd better stay."

He stayed four years. And then—because he did well enough, because Ben and Nancy thought well of him still—he went to the state college at Lexington. After two years, because he knew his own mind by then, and knew Margaret's, he wrote at the end of one of his letters home: "Pa, when I come back this June, I am going to stay." And Ben replied:

> My dear Mat,
>   You have grown to a man and a good one I think. I ask no more. Come ahead. Stay on. There is employment here for you as much as you can make yourself equal to. We are plowing as weather permits. We have two excellent mule foals from the gray mares. Your Ma is well and sends her love, as I do also.
>   Pa

It is early June of 1906, a sunny day. The little steamboat, *The Blue Wing*, has stopped, it seems to him, a hundred times, to unload a barrel of flour and a bolt of cloth at one landing, and at another, a mile downstream, to load a drove of hogs and two passengers, as unmindful of his haste as time itself.

At last he sees forming ahead of them, still blue with distance, the shape of the Port William hill, and then one of his father's open ridgetops, and then the steeple pointing up over the trees, and then the old elm at the landing. As the boat sidles in out of the current, he looks up and sees standing on the porch of the store above the road Margaret, who has loved him all his life until then, and will love him all the rest of it. She has heard the whistle and walked down to meet him. He waves. She smiles and waves back, and an old longing, the size of himself, opens within him.

He is moving toward the gangplank, the end of which is already poised over the bank. The boat is coming in only to put him off; it will not stop long enough to tie up. He is ready to step onto the plank when an old man who has been watching him hooks him with his cane.

"You're Ben Feltner's boy."

"Yessir."

The old man shakes his white beard in self-congratulation. "I sometimes miss the dam. I never miss the sire."

"Yessir."

"And your mammy was a Beechum."

"Yessir."

"Well, you got some good stock in you," the old man says, feeling his shoulder and looking him over. Oh, taking his time!

"You been up there to that college, my boy?"

"Yessir."

"Well, you'll be going away now, I reckon, to make something out of yourself."

Mat is stepping onto the plank, free now. "Nosir, I reckon not."

Margaret is coming down the bank to meet him, her long skirt gathered in one hand to keep it out of the dew.

"Now, here are your extra clothes. They're clean, and I've darned your socks. That sack's got your shaving things in it and some other odds and ends. And there's a check in there from your granddaddy for your wages, and I think maybe a little more."

Margaret has a list in her mind. Andy is going away to college, and she has been thinking, for days maybe, of what she must do and what she must say.

"Okay," he says. He would like to leave, for he knows that all these things signify her love for him, and he is going away, and she is sad, and he is.

"Now wait. I'm not finished. Inside that sack is a tin of cookies for you to take with you to school. Don't shake them and make crumbs out of them, and don't eat them before you get there. And when you do get there I want you to apply yourself and study hard, because I think you've got a good mind and it would be a shame to waste it. Your granddaddy thinks so too."

She pauses, thinking over the rest that she must say. Her eyes are on him, direct and grave behind her glasses. He cannot turn away or look away until she is ready for him to go. He is grinning but not, he knows, fooling her.

"Listen. There are some of us here who love you mighty well and respect you and think you're fine. There may be times when you'll need to think of that."

He has two thousand miles to go, and if he is going he must begin. He thinks of how far he has come, how many miles, how many steps. Some who came here came by steps, across prairie and desert and mountain, past the whitened bones of starved oxen and horses and mules, the discarded furniture and wrecked wagons, the stone-mounded graves of those who had come earlier and come no farther. He thinks of flying. At what risk and cost do the fallen fly?

Preserve me, O Lord, until I return. Preserve those I am returning to until I return.

When he does remove his elbows from the parapet where he has been leaning, and turns, and steps away, a history turns around in his mind, as if some old westward migrant, who had reached the edge at last and seen the blue uninterruptible water reaching out around the far side of the world, had turned in his tracks and started eastward again.

He walks along the pier, past the backs of the intent fishermen and the concrete benches and back onto land again. There are swimmers in the harbor, early sightseers standing and walking about, and on the walks of Aquatic Park joggers trotting in pairs and talking. He makes his way among them, in the hold of a direction now, stepping, alone and among strangers, in the first steps of a long journey that, by nightfall, will bring him back where he cannot step but where he has stepped before, where people of his lineage and history have stepped for a hundred and seventy-five years or more in an indecipherable pattern of entrances, minds into minds, minds into place, places into minds: the worn and wasted, sorrow-salted ground, familiar to him as if both known and dreamed, that owns him in a membership that he did not make, but has chosen, and that is death and life and hope to him. He is hurrying.

"Hey, man!"

Andy stops, astonished, for it is clear to him that he is being addressed, though he does not yet see by whom. And then he sees the fringed and shaggy man hurrying toward him out of a side street, the rolled bandanna around his head, his hand in the air.

"Say, good brother, could you, like, spare me a buck for a light lunch?"

"Hold on, now," Andy says. "Isn't this the same day it was this morning when I gave you six dollars?"

"Ah!" the man says. "Indeed!" He steps back a pace and makes the low bow of a cavalier, sweeping the pavement with the edge of his hand. "Pass, friend."

"Thanks, friend," Andy says. He hurries on.

The city encloses him now, the bay out of sight behind him. The streets are all astir, thousands of directions and purposes shifting and turning, meeting and passing, each making its way in the midst of the rest, colliding, turning aside, failing, succeeding, so that a man without a direction would be lost there and carried away. Ahead of him, up Columbus Avenue, the Transamerica Pyramid points up into an empty sky, so blue it makes his eyes ache.

He is hurrying. He is walking up Columbus Avenue on his way to Port William, Kentucky, but he is moving too in the pattern of a succession of such returns. He is thinking of his father.

Wheeler is on a train in the mountains west of Charlottesville, thinking of his father. It is a late evening in early summer. The sun is down, its light still in the sky. Wheeler's valise is in the rack over-head, his small trunk in the baggage car. Tomorrow morning he will get home. Marce will be at the station to meet him. Ordinarily he would come in the buggy, but tomorrow, because of the trunk, he will have the team and wagon. Wheeler is thinking of his father, and of tomorrow when they will ride together on the spring seat of the wagon through the tree-shaded lanes, looking at the country and at the light sliding over the sleek hides of the mules—five miles from the station at Goforth, through the sweet gap that Wheeler feels opened around him now between his past and his future, and then they will be home, and Dorie will have dinner ready. His thoughts force Wheeler suddenly to breathe deeply as if to make room for his heart to beat. He has the whole night ahead of him.

Later, he will go to the dining car for supper, and afterwards sleep, if he *can* sleep. Sleep will shorten the time.

Andy has tried before this to imagine his father as a young man. And now, without any effort or even forethought of Andy's, his father has appeared to him: a young man, eight years younger than he would be at Andy's birth, sixteen years younger than Andy is now, his face pleasant, lighted by humor, and yet his mouth and jaw are already firmed by a resolution that will be familiar to anyone who will know him later, and in his eyes there is already the shadow of effort and hard thought.

Wheeler was an apt and ambitious student who, after college, had been invited by the about-to-be-elected congressman from his district, Forrest Franklin, to go to Washington with him as his secretary. Wheeler accepted, on the condition that he would be permitted to attend law school as well. Mr. Franklin agreed to that, perhaps supposing that Wheeler would soon find the double load too much and would quit law school. Wheeler did not quit either one, and he did well at both.

By the time Wheeler's graduation was in sight, Mr. Franklin, who had become his friend, undertook to help him find employment. Mr. Franklin assumed, along with virtually every teacher Wheeler had ever had, that Wheeler's destiny was to be that of thousands of gifted country boys since the dawn of the republic, and before: college and then a profession and then a job in the city. This was the path of victory, already trodden out and plain. But Wheeler, to Mr. Franklin's great surprise, hesitated and put off. And one day Mr. Franklin called him in. The job in question was one with a large packing house in Chicago.

"Wheeler, you're an able young man. You've got the world in front of you. You can grow and develop and go to the top. You can be something your folks never imagined. You've got the ability to do it, Wheeler. And nobody will be prouder or delight more in your success than I will."

Mr. Franklin put both feet on the floor and leaned forward. He propped his right forefinger on Wheeler's knee.

"Wheeler. Listen. Don't, damn it, throw this opportunity away."

"Thank you, Mr. Franklin," Wheeler said, "I understand. I'll think about it."

He did think about it. He sat down at his desk and he thought. He thought of his mother and father who had skimped and denied themselves to send him to school. He asked himself what they had imagined he might become or do as an educated man, and he knew that they had imagined him only as he was, a bright boy and then a bright young man, deserving, they thought, of such help as they could give; for their help they wanted only his honest thanks, and they did not ask even for that. He knew that he could become what they had never imagined, and what he had never imagined himself. And he asked finally, thinking of them, but of himself too, "Do I want to spend my life looking out a window onto tarred roofs, or do I want to see good pastures, and the cattle coming to the spring in the evening to drink?"

Elation filling him, he answered, "I want to see good pastures and cattle coming to drink." For suddenly he did imagine what he could be. He saw it all. A man with a law degree did not have to go to Chicago to practice. He could practice wherever in the whole nation there was a courthouse. He could practice in Hargrave. He could be with his own.

He got up then and went back to Mr. Franklin's office. "Mr. Franklin," he said, "I'm going home."

And Mr. Franklin said, "WHAT?"

Andy knows how firmly ruled and how unendingly fascinated his father has been by that imagining of cattle on good grass. It was a vision, finally, given the terrain and nature of their place, of a community well founded and long lasting. Wheeler held himself answerable to that, he still holds himself answerable to it, and in choosing it he gave it to his children as a possible choice.

"It can inspire you, Andy," he said. "It can keep you awake at night. It doesn't matter whether you've got a manure fork in your hand or a library in your head."

"Look," he says, for he has brought Andy where he has brought him many times before, to the grove of walnuts around the spring, and the cattle are coming to drink. The cattle crowd in to the little stone basin, hardly bigger than a washtub, that has never been dry, even in the terrible drouth of 1930; they drink in great slow swallows, their breath riffling the surface of the water, and then drift back out under the trees. Andy and Wheeler can hear the grass tearing as they graze.

"If that won't move a man, what will move him? It's like a woman. It'll keep you awake at night."

Andy is old enough to be told that loving a place is like loving a woman, but Wheeler does not trust him yet to know what he is seeing. He trusts it to come to him later, if he can get it into his mind.

"Look," he says. And as if to summon Andy's mind back from wherever it may be wandering, for Andy's mind can always be supposed to be wandering, Wheeler takes hold of his shoulder and grips it hard. "Look. See what it is, and you'll always remember it."

What manner of wonder is this flesh that can carry in it for thirty years a vision that other flesh has carried, oh, forever, and handed down by touch?

Andy would like to know, for he is walking up Powell Street alone with the print of his father's hard-fingered, urgent hand as palpably on his shoulder as if the hand itself were still there. He is going past storefronts lined with fish, vegetables, and herbs, roasted ducks hanging by their necks in windows. He is hurrying among all the other hurriers, on his way to Port William.

Where is Port William? If he asked, who would know? But he knows.

He reaches the hotel and enters the lobby. It is all alight now with ordinary day. People are coming and going, standing around, sitting and talking. Reflected light from the passing traffic quivers and darts on the walls.

His room, once he has drawn the curtains back, is filled with ordinary daylight too, no longer the place of nightmare. His suffering of the night and early morning now has given way to a suffering of haste, distance, and mortality. He must get back before chance or death prevents him. He feels his frailty amid the stone and metal of the world crashing and roaring around him. He is praying to live until he can get home. To get there, he must pass a thousand ways to die. He has no time to waste. He bathes quickly, and shaves and combs his hair, looking at himself, it seems to him, for the first time in almost a year—a small, older, plainer man than he was before.

He puts on fresh underwear and shirt, and repacks his things into his small suitcase. And then he thinks of the hook, tempted at first to leave it.

No. Get it. It is only a tool.

It is not a hand. It is not a substitute for a hand. It is a tool, only a tool. His hand is gone. Sometime, somewhere behind him, his hand has left him. It has died, and is at peace.

5.

A Place Known and Dreamed

He pays his bill and goes out to wait on the curb for the airport limousine. He puts his bag between his feet and leans against a signpost as near the corner as he can get and yet be out of the way of the crowd. He is still now, gathered together, ready to go, and the city continues its coming and going around him.

He is a man fated to be charmed by cities. They frighten him and threaten to break his heart, but they charm him too. He came to them too late not to be charmed by them. The great cities that he has been to have exhilarated him by the mere thought of the abundance that is in them, not needing to be sent for.

Years ago, he resigned himself to living in cities. That was what his education was for, as his teachers all assumed and he believed. Its purpose was to get him away from home, out of the country, to someplace where he could live up to his abilities. He needed an education, and the purpose of an education was to take him away.

He did not want to go, and he grieved at night over his forthcoming long and distant absence. But no one he met at the university offered him reprieve. He could amount to something, maybe; all he needed was an education, and a little polish.

"For Christ's sake, Catlett," one of his professors told him in his freshman year, "try to take on a little *polish* while you're at it. You don't have to go through the world *alarmed* because other people don't have cowshit between their toes."

As it turned out, he did not take a very high polish. Polishing him was like polishing a clod of his native yellow clay; as soon as he began to shine, the whole glaze would flake off, leaving the job to be begun again.

After graduation he married, and went to San Francisco, where he worked as a journalist, a very minor journalist, covering minor rural and agricultural events. He learned a little of the way the agricultural world wagged, and, perhaps because he was so far from home and from what his father would have told him if he had asked, he assumed that the way it wagged was the way it was supposed to wag: that bigger was better and biggest was best; that people coming into a place to use it need ask only what they wanted, not what was there; that whatever in humanity or nature failed before the advance of this mechanical ambition deserved to fail; and that the answers were in the universities and the corporate and government offices, not in the land or the people. He was capable, in those days, of forgetting all that his own people had been. He loved them, he thought, but he had gone beyond them as the world had. He was a long way, then, from his father's ideal of good pasture, and from all that his old friend Elton Penn was and stood for and meant.

After three years in San Francisco, he went to Chicago to work for his university classmate and friend, Tommy Netherbough, who had become an editor of *Scientific Farming*. Tommy was from Indiana, a farmer's son, who openly despised what he called the "dungship" of his servitude, as a boy, to his father's antiquated methods. There were differences of attitude and affection between Tommy and Andy, but they lay dormant under Andy's assumption that Tommy was fundamentally right, and that his way was the way of the world. Tommy was a hard worker and he knew his business. As a student, he had known what he wanted to do, and once he was out in the world he began to do it, and to do well at it. Now, as an editor, he was better than ever. Andy liked him. They worked together for five years, and they got along. And then in the early spring of 1964 they had an argument that put them on opposite sides and changed Andy's life.

Andy went to Ohio to interview a farmer named Bill Meikelberger, who was to be featured in the magazine as that year's Premier Farmer. Meikelberger had caught Tommy Netherbough's eye because, like all the Premier Farmers before him, he was, as Tommy liked to put it, "one of the leaders of the shock troops of the scientific revolution in agriculture."

And Meikelberger was, in fact, out in front of almost everybody. He was a man, clearly, of exceptional intelligence, energy, and courage. He lived in the rich, broad land south of Columbus, where he farmed the two thousand acres he had acquired by patiently buying out his neighbors in the years since his graduation from the college of agriculture at Ohio State. He was the fulfillment of the dreams of his more progressive professors. On all the two thousand acres there was not a fence, not an animal, not a woodlot, not a tree, not a garden. The whole place was planted in corn, right up to the walls of the two or three unused barns that were still standing. Meikelberger owned a herd of machines. His grain bins covered acres. He had an office like a bank president's. The office was a carpeted room at the back of the house, expensively and tastefully furnished, as was the rest of the house, so far as Andy saw it. It was a brick ranch house with ten rooms and a garage, each room a page from *House Beautiful*, and it was deserted.

When Andy and Meikelberger had toured the farm and were going to the house for coffee, Meikelberger apologized for the absence of his wife.

"I'm sorry, too," Andy said. "Is she away on a trip?"

"She's in town at work."

"Oh, I see," Andy said, looking at Meikelberger.

"Every little bit helps," Meikelberger said.

There were only the two of them at home now. One of their children was a doctor in Seattle, one was in law school, one was married to a company executive in Moline.

The kitchen was large, modern, equipped with every available appliance, shiny, comfortable, and clean. Andy sat at the table while Meikelberger made coffee.

"Some kitchen," Andy said.

"Well, we don't use it much," Meikelberger said. "Helen went to work in town when our youngest child started school. With that and keeping the books here, she stays plenty busy. And I'm busy all the time. We don't do much housekeeping. We eat in town, mostly."

Andy sat with his notebook on the table in front of him, watching Meikelberger, and liking him, though Meikelberger was troubling him too. He kept making a few notes, knowing that he was not understanding everything yet.

Meikelberger was a heavy-shouldered, balding man, with a worried, humorous face. Andy had expected him to be proud of his farm, and he obviously was. He had recited readily, and with some pleasure, all the facts and figures Andy had asked for. But he also supplied, apparently with as much pleasure, a good many personal facts that were plainer and tawdrier than his production statistics.

Meikelberger poured their coffee and sat down. "There have been some changes here since my grandfather's time," he said. "He and my grandmother settled here on eighty acres, would you be-lieve that? They raised six children. We tore down the old house to build this one. Helen couldn't stand it, and I saw what she meant. It was a barn."

And then, as if to see what Andy would think, he turned to the glass doors, which opened onto the small backyard and bare fields, and, pointing, showed Andy the layout of the old farmstead: cellar and smokehouse, henhouse and garden, crib and granary and barn, all now disappeared.

"They'd be amazed if they could see this, wouldn't they?" Mei-kelberger waved his hand at the outside, where the little lawn be-came, without transition, a cornfield. "They'd think they were in another world."

"I guess they would," Andy said.

Meikelberger finished his coffee, pushed back his cup, and in-serted a large white tablet into his mouth, something that Andy had seen him do earlier.

"Are you sick, Mr. Meikelberger?"

"Ulcer acting up."

"I'm sorry. What's the cause of that?"

Again Meikelberger grinned. "You can't farm like this without having it on your *mind*."

"I'm sure you do have a lot to think about."

"Well, I've got hired help to keep track of, and machinery to keep running, and creditors to deal with, and so forth."

"You have creditors?"

"Hell yes! You know it as well as I do. Debt is a permanent part of an operation like this. Getting out of debt is just another old idea you have to junk. I'll never be out of debt. I never intend to be."

"I guess that's bound to keep your mind busy. But it sounds like your stomach would like some time off occasionally."

"You can't let your damned stomach get in your way. If you're going to get ahead, you've got to pay the price. You're going to need a few pills occasionally, like for your stomach, and sometimes to go to sleep. You're going to need a drugstore just like you're going to need a bank."

Andy did not learn anything from Meikelberger that surprised him, but he had not expected Meikelberger's frankness, which had afforded him more questions than answers. He drove away with a notebook full of figures, and many quotations and observations written in his private language of abbreviations, and some things in his mind that he would have trouble writing down in the language of *Scientific Farming*. The obstacle that now lay in his way was his realization, which Meikelberger himself had left him no room to avoid, that there was nothing, simply nothing at all, that Meikelberger allowed to stand in his way: not a neighbor or a tree or even his own body. Meikelberger's ambition had made common cause with a technical power that proposed no limit to itself, that was, in fact, destroying Meikelberger, as it had already destroyed nearly all that was natural or human around him.

The extent and gravity of the impasse Andy had come to was not immediately clear to him. He did not immediately admit to himself that he could not write the article on Meikelberger, but he did not go to work on it that night in the motel in Columbus, as ordinarily he would have, and he did not work on it the next morning. He had, as it turned out, a job for that day, but he did not yet know what it was.

That evening he was supposed to be in Pittsburgh, which left him a long half-day for work. But he did not work. He ate breakfast and then he started to drive. He drove eastward toward Pittsburgh, and as he did so it came clear to him that he did not want to get there in a hurry—that, in fact, he did not want to get there any sooner than necessary. He was in the hill country by then, and he began to ramble northward, taking the back roads. The character of the country had changed. The fields were smaller, the farmsteads were closer together, and there were many woodlands. He was meeting and passing buggies on the road. Presently he came to a grassed field between a woodland and a stream. Through the middle of the field a backfurrow had been freshly turned. It was a beautiful place, and as Andy slowed down to look at it a three-horse team appeared, coming around on the curve of the slope, drawing a plow. Andy pulled the car off the road and got out. The man riding the plow was bearded; he was dressed in black and wore a black broad-brimmed hat. Seeing Andy, he raised his hand. He drove on to the end of the furrow, raised the plow out of the ground, and stopped the team.

"Good morning!" he said, and his otherwise cheerful voice carried just a hint of a desire to know what Andy's business was.

Andy said, "You're not going to get anywhere very fast that way." And then he was sorry. It was what Meikelberger would have said.

But the man seemed not to mind. "Oh, they step right along," he said cheerfully. He had got off the plow and was now standing beside his furrow-horse with his hand on her neck. "They'll carry you over a lot of ground in a day." He smiled and looked at Andy. "But then, of course, you don't do more than you *ought* to."

There was something friendly and undisguised about the man. Though there was gray in his beard, his face was young. He was maybe ten years older than Andy. The openness and clarity of his countenance surprised Andy and yet seemed to offer some comfort to him. He realized that, without knowing this man at all, he trusted him. The team was made up of three large black mares. Andy wanted to be closer to them. He walked through the grass and dead weeds of the roadside to the fence.

"Do you breed your mares?"

"Those two have colts in the barn. This one"—the man patted

the neck of the mare next to him—"she's the grandmother. She took the year off." And then, seeing that Andy would like to come nearer, he said, "If you want to, step over the fence there at the post. That'll be all right."

Andy did so, and spoke to the horses and came and stood beside them with the Amishman. He asked about each of the mares and the man told him her breeding and history. The mares were excellent, Andy saw that, and he felt their strength and their patience.

"When I was growing up, we worked horses at home," he said. "Some horses, but mostly mules."

The man looked at him and smiled. "Well, maybe you would like to try these a round or two."

"Maybe you oughtn't to trust me," Andy said. "You don't know me."

"Oh, I see that you've been around horses. And these are gentle. Almost anybody can drive them."

"Well, my name is Andrew Catlett. They call me Andy." He put his hand out and the man took it.

"My name is Isaac Troyer."

Andy got onto the seat of the plow and took the lines into his hands, surprised at how familiarly he received them back again. He spoke to the horses, Isaac watching him, and turned them, and the grandmother mare stepped into the furrow on the other side of the land.

As he drove the long curve of the plowland, watching the dark furrow open and turn, shining and fresh-smelling, beneath him, Andy could feel the good tilth of the ground all through his body. The gait of the team was steady and powerful, the three mares walked well together, and he could feel in his hands their readiness in their work. Except for the horses' muffled footfalls and the stutter of the plowshare in the roots of the sod, it was quiet. Andy heard the birds singing in the woods and along the creek. How long had it been since Meikelberger had heard the birds sing? Meikelberger had no birds, except for the English sparrows that lived from his wasted grain, and even if he had had them he could not have heard them over the noise of his machines.

"How do you like them?" Isaac asked, as Andy raised the share at the furrow's end.

"I like them," Andy said.

"Well, drive them another round, if you want."

Andy drove them another round. This time, more at ease, he remembered something that as a child he had heard about, but now saw:

Mat, his grandfather, as a little boy, was sitting on a board that Jack Beechum had nailed to his plowbeam to make him a seat. As Jack walked behind the plow, Mat sat on the beam, and they talked. They talked about the pair of mules that drew the plow, and about the plow and how it was running, but they talked too about everything that a small boy could think to ask about, who had nothing to do but look and think and ask, except maybe, up in the afternoon, go to the spring to bring back a fresh drink of water in the gourd.

Was that a school? It was a school.

Andy thought of his own young children, who had descended, in part, from that school on the plowbeam, and did not know it. The mares strode lightly with their burden, the birds sang, the furrow rolled off the plow in a long, fluent motion, and a thrill grew in Andy at the recognition of something he wanted that he had forgotten.

At the end of the round, this time, Isaac Troyer took back his team. Andy, feeling awkward, said, "Look, I have an interest in farming. I like what I see of your place. Would you mind if I stay around a while?"

"Oh, well," Isaac said. "Oh, sure."

"Well, I thought I might like to walk around a little bit."

"Oh, sure. That's all right."

It was March, the air a little chilly, but the sun was warm. Andy walked along the creek to the end of the field, and then up along the fence through the band of woods on the steeper ground, the sprawled shadows of bare branches and the earliest flowers, and came out again on an upland, where he could see Isaac's house and barn and outbuildings.

He saw that the buildings were painted and in good repair. He saw the garden, newly worked and partly planted behind the house. He saw the martin boxes by the garden, and the small orchard with beehives under the trees. He saw fifteen guernsey cows and two more black mares in a pasture. He saw a stallion in a paddock beside the barn, and behind the barn a pen from which he could hear the sounds of pigs. He saw hens scratching in a large poultry yard. Now and then he could hear the voices of children. On neighboring farms, he could see other teams plowing. He walked as with his father's hand on his shoulder, and his father's voice in his ear, saying, "Look! Look!" He walked and looked and thought and wondered, and then he walked back down to the field that Isaac was plowing.

Isaac was unhitching the team. "Well, did you look around?"

"I did."

"Well, is this the kind of farm you're used to seeing?"

"It's not quite the kind I've been looking at. Would you mind if I asked you some questions about it?"

"Oh, I don't know." He spoke, as before, out of some good cheer, some satisfaction, some confidence that Andy was having trouble accounting for.

This was not one of the Premier Farmers that Tommy Netherbough held in such esteem. He was apparently less worried, for one

"Do you have work for everybody?"

"Oh, yes, plenty of work."

"For the old people and the little ones too?"

"Oh, yes, we need them all."

"You stay busy all the time?"

"We don't work on Sunday. Or after supper. Sometimes there's a wedding, or we go fishing."

Isaac watered his horses and fed them, and Andy went with him to the house. He met Anna, Isaac's wife, and Susan and Caleb, their two youngest children. He bowed his head with them over the food at the kitchen table. It was a clear, clean room. The food was good. A large maple tree stood near the back porch, visible from the kitchen windows, and the wind quivered in the new grass at its foot. Beyond were the white barn and outbuildings. It was a pretty place, its prettiness not so much made as allowed. It was a place of work, but a place too of order and rest, where work was done in a condition of acknowledged blessedness and of gratitude. As they ate, they talked, making themselves known to each other.

"Oh, *Scientific Farming*," Isaac said. "I've heard of that."

"No," Anna said. "You've seen it. Our neighbor gave us a copy once. I read it."

"Did it give any advice that you could take?" Andy asked.

"Some, maybe." She laughed. "Not much."

After dinner, taking Susan and Caleb along, Isaac and Andy walked over the little farm together, Andy questioning and, with Isaac's permission, writing down many of the answers. He learned about the various enterprises of the farm, about the exchanges of work within the neighborhood, about the portioning of work within the family, about the economies of household and homestead from which the family principally lived. Putting together what he heard and what he saw with what he knew already, Andy

thing. Andy thought of Meikelberger and his farm, a wa
culture as abstract as a graph or a statute or an airport.
thought of Isaac's place, which was, all of it, a home. It was
to many lives, tame and wild, of which Isaac's was on
and was so meant. There was something—Andy was try
words—something cordial or congenial or convivial ab
Whatever it was, it said that a man could live with trees and an
and a bending little tree-lined stream; he could live with neigh

And with strangers who happened by, too, for Isaac had
said, "Would you want to come eat? We got plenty."

"I'd hate to impose on you."

Isaac smiled at him. "Maybe you won't like what we got. It'l
plain."

"Plain will be lovely," Andy said. "Thanks."

And so he left the car by the road and walked beside Isaac, behir
the team, up through the woods to the barn, and on the way he que
tioned him.

"How much land do you have, Isaac?"

"Eighty acres."

"Eighty acres. Is that enough?"

"Enough for what?"

"To make a living."

"Well, we're living, aren't we?"

"How long have you been here?"

"Seventy-four years."

"But you're not seventy-four?"

"No," Isaac said, and laughed, "my father is seventy-four. We
came here the year he was born."

Isaac and his wife had five children, three in school and two little
ones still at home, and Isaac's father and mother lived in a small
house of their own a few steps from Isaac's.

began to see that these people lived very well on their eighty acres and with their neighbors, whose farms were all more or less the same size, and finally, uneasy but unable to resist, he asked point-blank, "Do you owe any money, Isaac?"

"Not for a while."

"Do you have any money saved?"

"Well, I better, hadn't I, with five children?"

"How much would you say you net in an average year?"

They looked at each other then, and both smiled in acknowledgment of the limit they were approaching.

"About half," Isaac said.

"Are all the Amish good farmers?"

"Some better than others. All the Amish are human."

By then Isaac was carrying Susan, who had gone to sleep as soon as he picked her up.

And then Andy told him about Meikelberger's farm. Had Isaac ever thought of buying more land—say, a neighbor's farm?

"Well, if I did I'd have to go in debt to buy it, and to farm it. It would take more time and help than I've got. And I'd lose my neighbor."

"You'd rather have your neighbor?"

"We're supposed to love our neighbors as ourselves. We try. If you need them, it helps."

"Have you ever thought of mechanizing the place you have?"

"What for? So my children can work in a factory?"

The horses were rested. It was time for Isaac to return to work and for Andy to be on his way. After taking the children to the house, they returned with the team to where they'd left the plow. They shook hands.

"Thanks," Andy said. "Thank you very much. I hope we'll meet again."

"That would be good," Isaac said. "Maybe we will. I'll be here."

In the middle of that afternoon, after Andy had been back on the main road a long time, all that he had learned in the last two days finally settled into place in his mind. He braked suddenly and again pulled over to the side of the road, for at last he had seen what was unmistakably the point: Twenty-five families like Isaac Troyer's could have farmed and thrived—could have made a healthy, comely, independent community—on the two thousand acres where Bill Meikelberger lived virtually alone with his ulcer, the best friend that the bank and the farm machinery business and the fertilizer business and the oil companies and the chemical companies ever had.

Andy sat for a long time then with his hands on top of the steering wheel and his head on his hands, and then he picked up a pad of paper from the seat beside him and outlined an article about Isaac Troyer. He would write it for his friend Rove Upperson, the only agricultural journalist he knew who would want to read it.

"Did you *really* think we could publish this?" Tommy Netherbough asked. He was sitting with one foot on the corner of his desk, holding the Isaac Troyer article with two fingers as if it were covered with mayonnaise.

Andy was sitting in a chair on the other side of the desk. He had understood that the dividing of ways had come when he received Tommy's peremptory note: "See me." Once in Tommy's office, he got the feeling that he was supposed to remain standing, as one who was outside the perquisites of friendship, and so he sat down.

"We're interested in successful farmers, aren't we?"

"I sent you to write on a successful farmer. Where the hell is the Meikelberger article?"

"If I wrote the truth about Meikelberger, you wouldn't publish that either."

"Meikelberger's the future of American agriculture."

"Meikelberger's the end of American agriculture—the end of the future. He's a success by way of a monstrous debt and a stomach ulcer and insomnia and the disappearance of a neighborhood. Isaac Troyer's the successful one of the pair, by any standard I know."

"Isaac Troyer is over and done with. He's as obsolete as the outdoor toilet. His farm is history, Andy. It's a museum."

"You mean you're against it."

"I'm not against it or for it. I can see that it's finished. We're not going to farm that way."

"You mean you don't *want* anybody to farm that way."

"I mean I don't want anybody to farm that way. You're letting nostalgia overrule your judgment. You've lost your sense of reality. What do you want, a job with *The Draft Horse Gazette*?"

"*The Draft Horse Gazette*—I'll have to find out about that."

"You should."

"I will."

The dividing of ways had come, but Andy made no move to get up. He was not arguing for himself now.

"What is this magazine trying to do—improve farming and help farmers, or sell agri-industrial products?"

Tommy sat looking at him, slowly nodding his head. He was angry now, Andy saw, and he did not care. He was angry himself. He was going to go. He had known it ever since the afternoon after his visit with the Troyers. He knew he was going; he did not yet know where.

Tommy said, "What you are, you know, is some kind of anarchist."

And then Andy knew what he was. He was not an anarchist. He was a throwback to that hope and dream of membership that had held together his lineage of friends and kin from Ben Feltner to himself. He was not arguing for himself, and not just for Isaac and Anna Troyer. He was arguing his father's argument. He was arguing for the cattle coming to the spring in the cool of the day, for the man with his hand on his boy's shoulder, saying, "Look. See what it is. Always remember." He was arguing for his grandparents, for the Coulters and the Penns and the Rowanberrys. And now he had seen that hope and dream again in Isaac Troyer and his people, who had understood it better and longer, and had gauged the threat to it more accurately, than anybody in Port William.

"Well," he said, looking at Tommy, trying to make his voice steady, "you do have to take an interest in your subscription list, don't you? You will have to consider, won't you, that more Meikelbergers will mean fewer farmers?"

After he spoke, he could hear the pleading reasonableness of his voice, and he regretted it.

Tommy looked at him in silence, still angry, as Andy was glad to see, and he let his own anger sound again in his voice. "Don't you have subscribers, for God's sake, whose interest is finally the same as your own? Don't you have a responsibility to your clients?"

"To hell with the subscribers! Listen! Let me give you a little lesson in reality. I don't know where you've been hiding your head. It's not subscribers that support this business—as you know damned well. It's advertisers. Our 'clients' are not farmers. They're the corporations that make the products that they pay us to advertise. We're not thinking in terms of people here. We're thinking in terms of blocks of economic power. If there are fewer farmers, so what? The ones that are left will buy on a bigger scale. The economic power will stay the same. A lot of farmers will buy little machines; a few farmers will buy big machines. What's the difference?"

Andy wanted to hit him. They were not even in the same argument that Andy had thought they were in. It was not an argument about right and wrong ways of farming. It was an argument about the way things were going to be for the forseeable future. And he was losing that argument. He was now on the side that was losing it, and he was furious. He felt his fury singling him out. And he was exultant. He stood, to discover that he was shaking.

For the foreseeable future, then, no argument would be effective against the blocks of economic power. Farmers were going to fail, taking the advice of Netherbough and his kind. And Netherbough and his kind were going to thrive, giving bad advice. And that was merely what was going to happen, until the logical consequences of that course of success became intolerable. And then something else would happen. And who knew what?

But that an argument was losing did not mean that it should not be made. It had already been made, and it would be made again, not because he would make it, but because it existed, it always had, and he belonged to it. He would stand up on it here, in Tommy Netherbough's office, in Tommy Netherbough's face. That it was losing did not mean it was beaten.

"We have a difference," he said. "You don't think Isaac Troyer represents anything that you and your readers ought even to consider?"

"I don't think he's even considerable."

"Do you know whose side I'm on, between you and Isaac Troyer?"

"I don't think you have such a choice."

"Well, I choose Isaac Troyer's side."

"Do you know what that choice will cost you?"

He knew. He was shaken, and shaking, but he knew. "It won't cost anything I can't pay."

He knew then where he was going. As he was leaving Tommy's office, it came to mind, all of a piece, a place familiar as if both dreamed and known: the stone house above the wooded bluff, the spring in its rocky cleft, the ridges, the patches of old woods, the smell of bruised bee balm in the heat of the day, the field sparrow's song spiraling suddenly up into the light on the ridgetop, the towhee calling "Sweet!" in the tangle.

He asked a secretary to get word to Flora that he had been called out of town and would be back tomorrow. And then he drove to the airport.

He is in the limousine, swinging in the curves of the freeway, heading south out of San Francisco toward the airport. His bag is under his feet, the other passengers are looking straight ahead, nobody has said a word. He is thinking of himself driving out of Chicago toward the airport, twelve years ago, his anger at Tommy Netherbough grown to a kind of elation, lifting his thoughts, and he was thinking of the Harford Place.

When they wanted to be very specific about it, they called it the Riley Harford Place. Riley Harford had died there in 1903, and his neighbor, Griffith Merchant, Ben Feltner's first cousin, had bought the hundred acres. In 1903 Griffith Merchant was on his last legs himself, but buying land was his habit, and when he got the chance he bought Riley Harford's. After Griffith's death in 1906, the Harford Place, along with the rest of the Merchant land, was jointly inherited by Roger, Griffith's son, and Griffith's daughter, Violet, who was living in Paducah. From 1906, the Harford Place, along with the rest of the Merchant land, declined until 1945 when Mat Feltner assumed guardianship of Roger, who had by then become *non compos mentis* by the agency of drink, silliness, idleness, and age. Mat kept it, at least, from declining any further until 1948 when Roger died and it fell into the managerial powers of a Louisville law firm hired by Violet, and then, after Violet's death, by her daughter, Angela, who lived in Memphis. And now Angela was dead, and her children had moved to sell the land, most of it to be divided for that purpose into its original tracts. Henry Catlett, Andy's brother, had been hired by the Louisville firm to oversee the sale of it.

Andy had known the place all his life. He had hunted over it many times, and had worked over it almost as many, for, in the 1950s, after the house had been vacated by its last tenants, Wheeler and Elton had rented it, plowed the whole arable surface of it, and sowed it all in alfalfa and bluegrass. They made hay and pastured cattle there for five or six years, until the heirs refused to rebuild the fence. After that, so far as Andy knew, the place had lain idle, growing weeds and bushes.

By the time he flew to Cincinnati, rented a car, and drove to Hargrave, it was long past dark. He ate a sandwich in Hargrave, and then drove up the Port William road, and turned onto the gravel road that went up Katy's Branch. At the mouth of the lane going up Harford Run, he hesitated. It had been a long time, he imagined, since anybody had been up that lane with a tractor, let alone an automobile. But the momentum that had carried him out of Tommy Netherbough's office was still upon him, and he did not let the car come all the way to a stop. He turned, and as he entered the lane immediately saw that he could not see. The lane was choked with tree sprouts, the tall dead stems of last year's weeds, vines, raspberry briars, and, underneath the rest, a thatching of dead grass. The headlights penetrated the tangle to about the length of his arm, but they showed him at least the hill slope on the righthand side, cut back to accommodate the little ledge of the road.

"Come on," he said to the car, accelerating a little to keep it boring in, while the brush rattled and scraped around it. He was just trusting the road to be there, and it kept on being there, approaching him as anxiety, passing beneath him as relief.

"Come on," he said. It seemed to him that the little car was surprised, not having been brought up to such work. And then he saw abruptly the trunk of a tree fallen across the lane at the height of the windshield, and he jammed the car to a stop.

He pushed in the light switch and killed the engine, and sat still while the violence of his entry subsided around him. He heard silence, and then the peepers shrilling along Harford Run. After a time he got out and began to walk.

He wished for a flashlight, but he had not brought one. He had brought nothing but himself. But there was light from the moon, and he knew the place. He knew it day and night, for he had walked and worked over it in the daytime, and had hunted over it at night with Elton and Burley Coulter and the Rowanberrys. He would be all right except for the briars, which he found only by walking into them; he would have to put up with that. He was hurrying. He wanted to see if the old house was still standing. He wanted to see if the roof still covered it.

He followed the lane up over a rise and then down again, and through the three little tree-ringed meadows that lay along Harford Run, the peepers falling silent as he passed, so that he could hear the creek tumbling in the riffles. The woods stood dark on the bluff above the creek. The meadows were weedy, but he could see his way, for the night shone and shone upon them. And then there was an opening in the trees on the bluff, and he followed the road up through it to where the road went level again. From there he could see the top of the great spreading white oak that stood by the house. And then he could see the house.

It was a low stone house, thick walled, with an ell—four rooms downstairs, and upstairs two low, dormered ones with sloped ceilings. He walked through the shadow of the tree and up onto the porch. The door, when he pressed it, did not resist at all, the latch broken. He went in, shut the door, and walked, feeling his way through the dark, damp, mouse-smelling air, to the back door and came out again. It was sound, he knew then; after all the years of use and misuse and abandonment, not a board had creaked.

He went and looked at the barn, which had swayed off its footings along one side, but was still roofed and probably salvageable. He walked into the driveway, smelling the must of old hay and manure, old use. He stood in the barn in the dark, looking out into the bright night through fallen-open doors at each end. Many had worked there, some he knew, some he had heard of, some he would never hear of. He had worked there himself—work that he had thought he had left behind him forever, and now saw ahead of him again.

He had begun to dream his life. As never before, he felt it ahead of him, not maybe, not surely, as it was going to be, but as it *might* be. He thought of it, longing for it, as he might have thought of a beloved woman, known and dreamed. He dreamed, waking, of a man entering a barn to feed his stock in the dark of a winter morning before breakfast. Outside, it was dark and bitter cold, the stars glittering. Inside, the animals were awaiting him, cattle getting up and stretching, sheep bleating, horses nickering. He could smell the breath and warmth of the animals; he could smell feed, hay, and manure. The man was himself.

He went out. He went past the house and under the tree again. Following only a path now through a fallen gate, he went farther along the slope, crossed a little draw and slanted down through the still sheen of the moonlight to where a shadowed notch opened in the hillside beneath another white oak as large and spreading as the one by the house. Again feeling his way, he went into the shadow and up into the notch. When the shadow seemed to hover and close around him, he felt with his hands for the cleft in the rock, and found it, and felt the cold water flowing out and the flat stone edging the water. He knelt and drank.

His hurry was over then. He walked, taking his time, around the boundary of the hundred acres. After he had done that he went back to the car and put on his overcoat and got in under the steering wheel again and slept. As soon as it became light enough to see, he started the car and backed it out of the lane.

When he walked into the house, his clothes fretted by briars, mud from the Harford Place still on his shoes, Flora was sewing.

"Flora," he said, suddenly frightened, as if he did not know her, as if he might have mistaken her entirely, "we're going home."

She looked at him with her mouth full of pins, and then she took them out. "Well, it's about time."

"Well, don't you think we should? I mean, don't you want to know what I'm talking about?"

"Sure."

6.

Bridal

He passes through the Gate of Universal Suspicion and is reduced to one two-hundred-millionth of his nation, admitted according to the apparent harmlessness of his personal effects. Or it is an even smaller fraction that he is reduced to, for all the world is here, coming and going, parting and greeting, laden with bags and briefcases, milling around piles of baggage, hurrying through the perfect anonymity of their purposes. And none may be trusted, not one. Where one may be dangerous, and none is known, all must be mistrusted. All must submit to the minimization and the diaspora of total strangeness and universal suspicion. The gates of the metal detectors form the crowd momentarily into lines, and send it out again, particled, into the rush of the corridor. Adrift, he allows himself to be carried into that eddying, many-stranded current.

A man to the love of women born, no specialist, he feels his mind tugged this way and that by lovely women. They seem to be everywhere, beautiful women in summer dresses beautifully worn, flesh suggesting itself, as they move, in sweet pressures against cloth. He lets them disembody him, his mind on the loose and rambling, envisioning unexpectable results, impossible culminations. What pain of loneliness draws him to them! As though ghostly arms reach out of his body toward them, he yearns for some lost, unreachable communion. *You. And you. Oh, love!* Loving them apart from anything that he knows, or might know, he is disembodied by them: no man going nowhere, or anywhere, his mind as perfectly departed from his life as a lost ghost, dreaming of meetings of eyes, touches, claspings, words. He hears their music, each a siren on her isle, and deep in his own innards cello strings throb and strum in answer. He goes by them bound to his own direction. They flow past each other in their courses, countenances veiled, as though eternally divided, falling. They will not sing to him.

It seems to him that he is one among the living dead, their eyes fixed and lightless, their bodies graves, doomed to hurry forever through the abstraction of the unsensed nowhere of their mutual disregard, dead to one another.

This is happening to my soul. This is happening to the soul of all the world.

All in the crowd are masked, each withdrawn from the others and from all whereabouts. The light of their eyes, the warmth of their countenances, the regard of their consciousness and thought, their body heat—all turned inward. And the faces of the women are the most closed of all. For fear. Lost to men by fear of men in the Land of Universal Suspicion. The good level look of their eyes lost.

The more he sees of them in this place, the less he can imagine them. Who are they? What are their names? Where are they going? Who loves them? Whom do they love? They appear and pass, singly, each in the world alone, the solitary end result of the meetings of all the couples that have made her, each the final, single point of her own pedigree.

And where is the dance that would gather them up again in the immortal ring, the many-in-one?

He has heard the tread of his own people dancing in a ring, the fiddle measuring time to them, a voice calling them, through the steps of change and absence, home again, the dancers unaware of their steps, which only the music, older than memory, remembered. Now that dance is broken, dismembered in the Land of Universal Suspicion, where no face is open to another. Where any may be dangerous and none may be trusted, all must live in conflict, the fire of the world's death prefigured in every heart.

Shall we disappear with our longing, dismembered, in the annihilating flame?

Spare us, O Lord, the logical consequence of our folly.

Here is the eye of the whirlwind of directions. These gathered here today, tonight will be in Tokyo, Delhi, Paris, Lima, where? Dead, perhaps, on an unseen mountainside? Or dead in the world's death? The long corridor stretches out ahead of him, a noplace to which all places reach, beyond the last horizon of the world.

Where now is the great good land? Where now the house under the white oak? Oh, cut off, cut off!

A woman is walking ahead of him whose face he will never see. She is wearing a simple dress that leaves it to her to have the style. And she has it. How he would like to go up and walk beside her! How he would like to walk with his arm around her! He can imagine such a permission coming to him from her as would darken and stagger him as if blindfolded and turned round three times.

He will never see her again. He will never see her face. The dance that would bring her back again is broken. The hand that he would open to her is gone.

When he returned, bringing Flora and their children to live at the Harford Place, he returned to a country in visible decline. After his absence, he saw his native place as by a new birth of sight, and rejoiced in it as never before. But now he saw it also as a place of history—a place, in part, the result of history—and he began to see the costs that history had exacted: hillsides senselessly cropped, gullies in old thicket-covered fields that would not be healed in ten times the time of their ruin, woodlands destructively logged, farms in decline, the towns in decline, the people going to the cities to work or to live. It was a country, he saw, that he and his people had known how to use and abuse, but not how to preserve. In the coal counties, east and west, they were strip-mining without respect for the past or mercy to the future, and the reign of a compunctionless national economy, though most violent in the coal fields, was established everywhere, only a few daring to speak against it. Andy began to foresee a time when everything in the country would be marketable and everything marketable would be sold, when not one freestanding tree or household or man or woman would remain. Such thoughts, when they came to him, shortened his breath and ached in the pit of his stomach. Something needed to be done, and he did not know what. He turned to his own place then—the Harford Place, as diminished by its history as any other—and began to ask what might be the best use of it. How might a family live there without reducing it?

He has come to the second gate now, that between earth and sky, where his plane is waiting. He goes into the waiting lounge and chooses a seat against the end wall where he can see everything. He is sure that he will see nothing that will be of any use to him, but he is an economizer of opportunities.

Directly across from him is a man in a Palm Beach suit, with rings on the ring fingers of both hands, hidden from the lap up behind a newspaper proclaiming: TRANSVESTITE'S LIFE ENDS IN SHOOTING. Next there is a young couple—a young man in an army private's uniform, a young woman in T-shirt and jeans—who sit holding hands and do not speak. Beside them is a woman of perhaps sixty, in half-glasses, knitting a sweater, the yarn traveling upward in jerks from her large handbag. And beside her is a professional football player with his leg in a cast, chewing gum rapidly and reading a copy of *Keyhole* magazine. His showpiece lady is clinging to his arm, unattended. His injured leg propped on two pieces of leather luggage, the football player is wearing a warm-up suit with his team's famous name in block letters on the jacket. People recognize him and stare at him as they pass.

At the other end of the row, divided by an empty seat from the man with the newspaper, a woman in a tailored suit is sitting with a legal pad on her lap. She is talking to a tiny machine that she holds in her hand. She speaks, snaps off the machine to think, snaps it on again and speaks. She speaks almost inaudibly, but otherwise seems oblivious of the crowd around her. It is a wonder that she is of the same species and sex as the football player's lady, and yet both seem to have themselves in mind as types—symbols, perhaps, of historical epochs or phases of the moon. The businesswoman is austerely tailored and coiffured; her eye-glasses are severe. She lives, her looks imply, entirely by forethought, her beating heart nobody else's business. Her taste and bearing are splendid. She is impeccable.

And Andy would like to give her a little peck on her ear. His mind is calling out to her: "Hello, my Tinkerbelle, my winsome, weensy crocodile. Come out! Come out! I know you're in there somewhere."

He says to his mind, "Shut up, you dumb bastard!"

And yet he cannot take his mind or eyes from her, for she is very beautiful. And who is she? Where did she come from? Where is she going? He knows that he is looking at her across an abyss, that if all the world should burn, they would burn divided in its flames. She is wearing the veil of American success, lost in the public haze that has obscured the countryside. All lives, creatures, connections are hidden in it, all cries and songs silenced in its deserted speech. He is lost there himself, divided and burning. How would they break the veil? How call out?

O exile, for want of you, what night is cold, what stream is dry, what tree unleaved?

"*Ladies* and gentlemen, thank you for waiting. Flight 661 *has* now been accessorized, and is ready *for* passenger boarding *through* the jetway *at* gate eleven. We *would* like first to preboard those passengers requiring assistance *in* boarding and those *with* young children."

There is a small stir now among the waiting passengers. The wingless are preparing to fly. Andy feels the first clench of the difference between earth and air. The woman knitting looks up and looks back down again. The football player hands his magazine to his lady without looking at her, and stands. She puts the magazine into her purse, hands him his crutches, and follows him to the door, carrying their bags. Even on crutches and hampered by the unwieldy cast, he moves gracefully. His grace and bearing and a certain neatness of conformation have deceived Andy about his size. It is only when noticed point by point, neck and shoulder and arm, that the mass of the man becomes evident. He weighs maybe two hundred and fifty pounds, and yet he moves and places himself with a light and easy precision. His hands too are precise, as if alert to catch a flying bird.

Presently, the voice in the air wishes the other passengers to begin boarding. It asks those in the back rows of the plane to be seated first.

The beautiful businesswoman puts her pad of paper and her recording machine back into her briefcase. The man with the newspaper refolds it and puts his glasses in his shirt pocket. The soldier and his weeping girl stand up and hold each other tightly.

As their rows are called, they get up stragglingly and join the line at the door. They do not look at one another, each remaining in a separate small capsule of air, observing scrupulously the etiquette of strangers, careful lest by accident they should touch. The uniformed stewardess taking their boarding passes gives them each a smile made for strangers. "Thank you!" she says. "Thank you! Thank you! Thank you!" As Andy passes and goes on down the quaking tunnel toward the plane, he can smell the stench of engine exhaust and spilled fuel. The line moves to the door of the plane in little nudging advances that begin at the front and move back along its length to the rear, as an earthworm moves. Andy enters the door in his turn, and the halting movement of the line continues, branching into the aisles of the huge plane. Many are already in their seats, some reading newspapers, some opening their briefcases to go to work.

He says to himself, as he always does, "It is like a bus or a train. People take it for granted, and are at ease in it. Millions of people do this without death or injury. It is safer than driving a car. It is an ordinary thing."

But, also as he always does, he begins to argue with his first proposition: "It is too big. It is like a lecture hall. It is preposterous. And it is *most* extraordinary that humans should fly. They have done so only recently, and they do so only clumsily, with a ludicrous hooferaw of noise and fire. Human flight, after all, is only a false and pathetic argument against gravity, which has the upper hand and is the greater fact. All will come down. And some will fall."

A stewardess stands leaning against a bulkhead with her hands behind her back, saying, "*Good* morning! *Good* morning!"

He can smell the chemical smell of the plane, the disinfected cleanness of something that, though not new, is meant always to seem new. It is not marked either by its makers or its users. It will not wear like stone or wood and grow more beautiful. It is purely the result of design, purely answerable to function. All its flaws are secret, lying in wait in the imperfect attention and responsibility of human beings, in the undiscovered wear or breakage of some bolt or bearing or little wire.

He finds his seat next to a window on the left side of the plane, sidles in, and sits down. The aisles remain full of people coming in, finding seats, stowing luggage. In the seat across from Andy, a businessman has his opened briefcase on his lap. He is holding a sheaf of invoices in his left hand, and with his right hand is working rapidly a small calculator, a pencil crosswise in his mouth. And now a very pretty young lady, a very pleasant, intelligent-looking lady, nicely made, stops beside Andy. She opens the overhead compartment and lifts her suitcase. It is heavy, and she struggles with it.

"Can I help you?" Andy says.

"No," she says. "But thanks."

She puts the bag into the compartment, and he is relieved. He did not want her to see that he has lost his hand, a fact which he now disguises by folding his arms, the stumped arm beneath the good one. She settles herself in the seat next to him, makes herself comfortable and orderly with little attentions to her clothes. Like other women alone in such places, she is enclosed within herself, not wary perhaps, but composed with a composure that certainly includes the possibility of wariness. She takes from her purse a book, *Beyond the Hundredth Meridian*, and opens it and begins to read. It is a book that Andy knows, by a writer he loves, and he almost speaks to her about it, but he does not. He does not want her to be wary of him. It seems to him that he could not bear for her to be wary specifically of him.

The travelers are all in their seats now. There is a click and an unlo-
catable aerial voice says, "*Ladies* and gentlemen, our destination
today *is* Cincinnati *and* Cincinnati *only*. *If* Cincinnati is not *your*
destination, please *do* deplane the aircraft." There is another click,
and presently the sound of the door closing, the outside noise suddenly excluded, the inside noise suddenly contained, and they are
sealed within the possibility of flight, committed to the air.

We commit these bodies to the air, O Lord, and to Thy keeping.

The plane lurches and rolls back from the gate and turns, brakes,
lurches, and begins its trip out to the runway. The passengers all
move as it moves, lurch as it lurches, all enveloped now in the one
power.

A stewardess stands at the head of the aisle, and another at the
head of the aisle on the other side of the plane, and as the disembodied voice explains their movements, these two act out the ritual pan-
tomime of survival in the breathless heavens, salvation in the midst
of danger: how to fasten the seatbelt, when to refrain from smok-
ing, how to don the oxygen mask, how to find the exits.

"This voice is talking about *falling*," Andy thinks. "It is talking
about breathing oxygen while we fall. It is talking about finding the
exits after we have fallen. That is why the voice is from the air,
disembodied."

The plane waits in the line of planes waiting to take off. It stops
and starts, moving around slowly to the end of the runway. When
its turn comes, it leaps forward, roaring, jolting, and shuddering
with its sudden commitment to flight. It lifts and rises. Going up
through the lower, warming layers of the air, it bucks and tosses like
a little boat in waves. Andy braces his feet against the legs of the seat
in front of him and holds tight to the arm of his seat, panicked, as
always, to feel that there is nothing to hold to that is not in the air.

When the air becomes smooth, he can think again. He becomes
aware, with a kind of wonder, of the unconcern around him. The

people who were reading newspapers are still reading them. The young woman sitting next to Andy has not looked up from her book. He looks at the page she is reading and finds John Wesley Powell's sentence: "I feel satisfied that we can get over the danger immediately before us; what there may be below I know not."

Afloat in fickle air, laboring upward, the plane makes a wide turn out over the ocean, and heads inland. Andy can see the city with its bridges, the Marin peninsula, and, even farther below, the upper part of the bay, and then the marshes of the river delta. As they rise from it, the details of the ground diminish, draw together, and disappear. The land becomes a map of itself.

To Andy, the air is an element as dangerous to mind as to body. For wingless creatures, it is the element of abstraction: abstract distance and speed, abstract desire. Flight seems to him to involve some radical disassemblement, as if one may pass through it only as a loose suspension of particles, threatened with dispersal.

"Ladies and gentlemen, this is your captain speaking. We want to welcome you aboard, and thank you for flying with us. We're ascending now to our cruising altitude of 37,000 feet. Our route today will carry us approximately over Denver, Salina, Kansas, Springfield, Illinois, Indianapolis, and then on down to Cincinnati. Our flying time will be, oh, about three hours and fifty-three minutes. As soon as we have reached altitude, our cabin attendants will be around with complimentary beverages and lunch. So settle back, folks. Enjoy your flight."

Thirty-seven thousand feet is over seven miles. How long would it take to fall seven miles? He thinks of falling seven miles and knowing that one is falling. Flight has always returned him to the ancient desire to die at home. He does not want to die in some place of abstraction, or in a featureless heap in some place he has never seen. But he fears most his body's brutal fear of falling, of falling through the high and alien air and knowing it. He imagines the moment before the crash when the body, remembering its long familiarity with itself, would find it strange. His hand, that had imagined many things, had never imagined its absence.

He wonders, if they were going down, would the young woman sitting beside him be willing to hold his hand? He looks at her, covertly, wondering. Holding hands, they would go down through the miles of air and crash into their total absence from the earth forever. She catches him looking, lifts her chin a little, and tugs down the hem of her skirt.

"Now you've done it!" he thinks. "You'll have to crash by yourself."

They cross the patchwork of farmland in the valley, and then the foothills, golden under the dark green oaks. And then the forests begin, and the bright gray rock of the Sierra Nevada, snow on the higher summits. Yosemite Valley, under a flock of little clouds, opens deep in the stone. Andy thinks of the islands of wilderness, bypassed in settlement, now tramped by modern backpackers, starved for what has been destroyed elsewhere and what their economy is destroying everywhere. Over it all hangs the brown veil of the world's entrails lifted up and burned.

Spare us, O Lord, the logical consequence of our folly.

Out his window he can see the huge engine shuddering under the wing. The cabin is flooded with light. They are flying in the pure sky, corrupted only by their flight, and below that is the smutted sky, and below that the world, that cannot be helped except by love.

They are flying above white, flat-bottomed clouds sailing eastward, their shadows dark on the treeless red hills of Nevada.

Among the hills there is a large lake, blue as the sky. The streams curve sweetly against the curves of the land. The older roads follow the streams, curving with them. The newer, larger roads are ruled according to the ideal of flight, deferring as little as possible to the shapes of the land. And above it all is the veil of the smog, and above the smog this little room in the air, on the long stem of its seven-miles-fallen shadow, depending for life on speed and fire, on the ability of an explosion to sustain itself for three hours and fifty-three minutes.

Andy is one of the last to receive his lunch: a plastic tray containing a tossed salad, an empty coffee cup, a helping of roast beef with gravy, small carrots, and a potato, a piece of chocolate cake, a tiny paper carton of pepper and one of salt, a plastic envelope containing a knife, a fork, a spoon, and a napkin.

Andy tears the envelope of salad dressing with his teeth and squeezes the contents onto his salad, needing another hand for this operation, but finally succeeding approximately; and then he begins the struggle to liberate his silverware.

The stewardess, pausing in the aisle with a pot of coffee, watches him a moment with unseemly absorption—a one-handed man in the toils of supraterrestrial sanitation—and then, leaning solicitously toward him, asks, "Does everything seem to be all right, sir?"

"Well, as long as we are supposing, let us suppose so."

"I beg your pardon, sir?"

"I'm sorry," he says, "I was joking. Everything seems to be all right. Thank you."

She returns to her distance and her smile. "Enjoy your meal, sir."

They eat and drink, pretending to be groundlings who are pretending to fly, trays in front of them laden with food and drink that will leave a plastic residue to be thrown away in some place out of the sight of groundlings pretending to be clean, the country below them become a map, perhaps not even of itself.

What there may be below I know not.

There comes over Andy a longing never to travel again except on foot, to restore the country to its shape and distance, its smells and looks and feels and sounds.

Spare us, O Lord, the logical consequence of our ingratitude.

Remember not, Lord, our offences, nor the offences of our forefathers.

The stewardesses have taken the trays away. Utah is below them now, canyon country, eroded yellow and pinkish walls opening among sparsely forested slopes. Andy is thinking of the wagons laboring westward against the resistant shapes of the land, places supplanting places. Of the one-armed Powell and his men on the Colorado, living by intelligence and strength and will alone.

How many connecting strands are braided there in the passes and the fording places, to be dissolved out of mind and lost almost before the grass could grow again over the wheel tracks, almost before the rain could wash them away?

I should walk. I should redo every step. It is all to be learned again.

"Andy, here's something you ought to see," Burley Coulter says, handing him a page, folded and worn, brown with age, the ink on it brown. Burley is sitting in his chair by the stove in the living room with a shoebox open on his lap.

Flora is there too, and Danny and Lyda Branch, their children playing among the chair legs, returning now and again to the large bowl of popcorn that Lyda is holding. Outside, the wind is blowing and it has started to snow. Andy and Flora have already said twice that they need to be going, but Burley has kept on taking things from the box and handing them to Andy, who has examined them and passed them on to Flora, who has passed them on in turn to Lyda and Danny. They do not remember what reminded Burley of the box. At some point in their conversation he remembered it, and went up the stairs to his room and got it. He set it on his lap, untied the heavy string that was around it, and began to probe into it with his crooked, big-knuckled forefinger. The box contains his keepsakes—the family's from long back, but his because after his mother's death he continued to keep them and to add to them the odd relics of his own life that he could not bring himself to part with. There were some photographs, a few letters, a gold watch, Spanish and French coins carried back along the footpaths from New Orleans in the pockets of Coulter men who had made the downward trip on flatboats or rafted logs. These had all been looked at and explained so far as Burley could explain them. And then from the very bottom of the box he brought up the folded brown page.

"Boys," he says, "your great-great-grandmother wrote that. She was married to another Nathan Coulter. Way back yonder. She was a McGown. Letitia. Letitia McGown. Read it, Andy. My eyes have got so I can't make it out."

And so Andy reads the script, not much used since it was a schoolgirl's, of an old woman dead before the Civil War:

"Oh that I should ever forget We stood by the wagon saying goodbye or trying to & I seen it come over her how far they was a going & she must look at us to remember us forever & it come over her pap and me and the others We stood & looked & knowed it was all the time we had & from now on we must remember We must look now forever Then Will rech down to her from the seat & she clim up by the hub of the wheel & set beside him & he spoke to the team She had been Betsy Rowanberry two days who was bornd Betsy Coulter 21 May 1824 Will turnd the mules & they stepd into

the road passd under the oak & soon was out of sight down the hill
The last I seen was her hand still raisd still waving after wagon &
all was out of sight Oh it was the last I seen of her that little hand
Afterwards I would say to myself I could have gone with them as
far as the foot of the hill & seen her that much longer I could have
gone on as far as the river mouth & footed it back by dark But how-
ever far I finaly would have come to wher I would have to stand and
see them go on that hand a waving God bless her I never knowd
what become of her I will never see her in this world again"

They have passed the snowfields of the Rockies, Denver under its
pall, and now in their orient flight are passing above a great floor
covered with newly sheared fleeces shining in the sun, sight going
down through it, where it thins, into shadow, the shadowed world,
diminished, thirty-seven thousand feet below.

Now it comes back into his mind, that country, green and folding, that he knows as his tongue knows the inside of his mouth. It
appears to him as if from the air, as in fact he remembers seeing it
from the air, when a plane he was on happened to fly over it. He saw
it then, he thought, as it might appear to the eye of Heaven, and
afterwards was obliged to see himself and his life as small, almost
invisible, within the countryside and the passage of time.

He sees Elton's old truck rocking and jarring over the humps and
holes of the Katy's Branch road on the way to the Harford Place
early in the morning. He and Henry and Elton are in the cab. He is
sitting between Elton and Henry. Elton is driving. He sees the countryside shadowy and dewy under the misty light; he sees the road
and the truck and the three of them in the cab littered with tools,
ropes, spare parts, and other odds and ends that they have grown
used to or may need. Henry is holding the water jug on his lap to

keep it from turning over. He has been telling about his date of the night before for the edification of Elton, who has been egging him on by protesting that *he* would never have thought of anything like that, not him.

Elton says, "What did you do last night, Andy?"

"I stayed at home."

"You run out of girls?"

"Yes."

"Well, you need to find one that's not too smart, old pup."

Henry says, "*Duh*, kiss me, old pup."

And Andy says, "Shut. Up."

Henry makes his hands quiver. "Sometimes. He causeth me. To tremble."

"I told you."

"He giveth me. Trembolosis. Of the lower. Bowell."

Elton is enjoying this, but he knows he won't enjoy it long. "I'll causeth you to tremble in a minute. *Both* of you shut up."

He sings with raucous sorrow two lines of "Blue Eyes" as a comment on Andy's girl-lessness, and gives a long raucous squall as a comment on yodeling. They laugh and go on up the lane, happy, the old truck creaking and rattling, the day brightening.

Andy can see the three of them jolting along over the bumps of the road—no blacktop on it then—overgrown with trees, a tunnel. It is as though he is standing in the air, watching, and at the same time an unseen fourth person in the cab. And he is moved with tenderness toward them and with love for them.

They come to the bright field, the stand of alfalfa nearly perfect on it, and Elton stops beside the two tractors where they left them the evening before. They fill the gas tanks and check the oil. They make the necessary small repairs on the mowing machines and grease them.

Elton says, "All right. You're ready to go. Be careful. If the hay you cut day before yesterday is dry enough by ten-thirty or eleven o'clock, Henry, you quit mowing and hitch to the rake. I'll be back to get you at dinnertime."

And then, looking up at Henry, who is standing on the truck bed, looking down at him, he says, "Get off of there now, damn it, and get started."

Henry takes three steps and does a handspring off the truck bed and lands standing up in front of Elton, who has to grin in spite of himself. "I wonder," he says. "Sometimes I wonder."

That was an island in time, between the horse and mule teams and the larger, more expensive machines that came later. They were not going to live again in a time like that.

The Harford Place appealed to Elton and touched his imagination, and he made them see it as he saw it.

"Listen," he said to Andy once—they had brought sandwiches with them that day and were eating in the shade by the spring—"do you see what this old place is? The right man could do something here. It's been worked half to death and mistreated every way, but there's good in it yet." He gestured up toward the house and barn. "That's still a sound, straight old house. The barn's not much, but it could be put right and made into something."

He had been thinking about it all morning, Andy knew, studying it as it was, foreseeing it as it might be, and now was telling him about it, because, though Elton knew that he would never make it over himself, he wanted *somebody* to do it.

"Listen, Andy," he said, "if you could find the right girl, a little smarter than you, and willing to work and take care of things, here's where you could get started and amount to something. Put some sheep here. A few cows. I'd help you, and the rest of them would, we'd neighbor with each other and get along."

And so Andy had the old place in mind, as it was and as it might be made, long before it ever occurred to him that he might be the one to live there and attempt to make it as it might be.

For that to happen required, in fact, the right girl, but also many miles, many happenings, and several years.

And it required trust. He sees it now. What he and Flora have made of the Harford Place has depended all on trust. They have not made it what it might be—how many lives will it require for that?—but they have made it far more than it was when they came to it. In twelve years they have given it a use and a life; a beauty has come to it that is its answer to their love for it and their work; and it has given them a life that belonged to them even before they knew they wanted it. And all has depended on trust. How could he have forgotten? How could he have failed to understand?

His life has never rested on anything he has known beforehand—none of it. He chose it before he knew it, and again afterwards. And then he failed his trust and his choice, and now has chosen again, again on trust. He has made again the choice he has made before, as blindly as before. How could he have thought that it would be any different? How could he have imagined that he might ever know enough to choose? As Flora seems to have known and never doubted, as he sees, one cannot know enough to trust. To trust is simply to give oneself; the giving is for the future, for which there is no evidence. And once given, the self cannot be taken back, whatever the evidence.

He sees again the long room, the librarian at her desk, tall shelves of books all around the walls, the double row of heavy oak tables with shaded lamps—a place where two ways met. He sees as from the penumbra above the shelf tops the eight students at the table in the farthest corner of the room: Flora, Hal Jimson, Ted Callahan,

Norm Leatherwood, himself, and three others. They are most of Professor Barton Jones' class in the history of the American Revolution. Professor Jones, known beyond his own earshot as Black Bart, is legendary for his freshman history classes, which terrorize even those freshmen who do not take them. The eight at the table are not freshmen, and they are not terrified; but the midterm examination is approaching, and they are properly intimidated. Professor Jones regards the teaching and learning of American history as a matter of desperate emergency. Day after day he has stood in his classroom in his portentous bulk, glowering upon them, thumbing his text with his great thumb, or beating with a pointer for emphasis upon a blackboard perfectly blank. That he loves the people he is teaching about, or some of them, only a little on the critical side of idolatry, and that he is capable of the most generous kindness to those whom he is teaching, they all know. And yet they are intimidated. For they know too the simple ferocity with which he regards their least proclivity to misunderstand or forget. They have been trying to make fluent their understanding of the development and the influence of the mind of Thomas Jefferson. They know that they are going to have to deal convincingly with that on the midterm, and again on the final.

It is late. The room is almost empty. The quiet in the room has begun to communicate with the quiet of the dark trees outside. One by one, Black Bart's little clutch of students disperses, having attained either confidence or resignation. Now only Andy and Flora remain, Andy at the foot of the table and Flora two chairs away. With each departure it has become harder for Andy to think about Thomas Jefferson, and now he is not thinking about Thomas Jefferson at all. He is thinking about Flora, who is still at work, bent over her book and notebook. Andy is not at work, though he is pretending to be. He is looking at his book and thinking about Flora, from time to time raising his eyes over the top of the book to look at her, to see if external reality lives up to the image in his mind, realizing, each time with a clench in his chest very like pain, that it does. For a college girl of the time, she is plainly dressed: a gray skirt, a white blouse with little buttons, open at the throat, a black un-buttoned cardigan. Except for perhaps a touch of lipstick, she wears no makeup, and needs none, and no jewelry, and needs none. Above her preoccupied face, her dark curls are rejoicing on their own.

He can see nothing wrong with her. She has closed entirely the little assayer's office that he runs in his mind. She seems perfect to him, and there is something about her, something beyond her looks, something that he calls "something about her," that has un-steadied whatever square yard of ground or floor he happens to be walking or standing on.

Such joy and pain are in him to be so near her, alone with her, permitted to look at her, that he can hardly breathe. It seems to him that apart from her he can no longer breathe. It seems to him that if he does not speak to her he will stop breathing. If he speaks, he knows, everything is going to change, into what he does not know.

He says, hardly above a whisper, his heart crowding so into his throat, "Flora, do you want to come here for just a while?"

She smiles and looks up at him with a look that she will give him again, amused a little, perhaps, but not surprised; it is a look that suggests to him, in his alarm, that she never has been surprised in her life.

He cannot deny her. Her eyes as they were then are on him now, and as they were when he saw them last, hurt and angry, full of tears. He cannot meet her eyes. It has been a long time since that night when she first looked at him, her face open to him, her eyes unguarded. It has been twenty years. He knows their duality in those years, the imperfection of them both, the grief and longing of their imperfection. And yet it is her justice that he feels now. He cannot meet her eyes that give his eyes such pain he cannot raise or open them. He has been wrong. His anger, his loneliness, his selfish grief, all have been wrong. That she, entrusted to him, should ever have wept because of him is his sorrow and his wrong. He sits with his head down, his eyes burning, such fire of shame covering him that he can hardly hold himself in his seat.

He knows she is right. He must have her forgiveness. He must forgive himself. He must forgive the world and his own suffering in it.

Have mercy upon me, O God, after thy great goodness; according to the multitude of thy mercies do away mine offences.

He must have his own forgiveness and hers and the children's, and the forgiveness of everyone and every thing from which he has withheld himself.

Thou shalt make me hear of joy and gladness, that the bones which thou hast broken may rejoice.

Now she comes to him again. He can see her again: a bride, dressed all in white, as innocent as himself of the great power they were putting on, frightened and smiling—a gift to him such as he did not know, such as would not be known until the death that they would promise to meet together had been met, and so perhaps never to be known in this world.

The way is open to him now. Thanks, as if not his own, shower down upon him.

"Are you all right?"

It is the young woman sitting next to him, who to his astonishment is patting his arm.

"Yes. I've been all right before, and I'm all right now."

7.

The Hilltop

Returned from the sky, his shadow attached to him again, Andy unlocks the door of his old pickup, slides the suitcase in across the seat, and climbs again into the aura of his workdays: the combined essences of horse sweat, man sweat, sweated leather, manure, grease and oil, dirt. He opens the windows to let out the trapped hot air, starts the engine, which roars loudly through its leaky muffler, drives to the booth, pays the girl in the glass enclosure, and heads for the interstate, hurrying again, but being careful.

He passes through the swoop of the entrance ramp, and is at once hurtling along in four lanes of roaring traffic that seems to have been speeding there forever. He speeds along with it, being careful, eternity gaping all around him. He drives like a messenger entrusted with a message that at all costs he must deliver. The message, it seems, is only himself. When he arrives he will have some things to say, he will have to say some things, but he does not yet know what.

But he is not trying to think of words now. He is thinking about being careful, the bright crustaceans speeding all around him along the road, each enclosing its tender pulp of flesh, creatures of mud and light, each precious beyond telling for reasons never to be known to the others, already dead to one another in mutual indifference. If one of those particles erred in its flight, then an appalling innovation would occur, an entrance to another world mauled through the very air and light. He is praying to remain in time until what he owes is paid.

The eight lanes of the interstate become six and then four. The traffic thins. The city is behind him now, except for the road itself that is the city's hardened effluent, passing through its long gouge without respect for what was there before it or for what is now alongside it. The road reminds him, as it always has before, of the power of words far removed from what they are about. For the road is a word, conceived elsewhere and laid across the country in the wound prepared for it: a word made concrete and thrust among us.

He knows that he is not yet beyond the spell of the unpeopled language that emanates from conference rooms and classrooms and laboratories and offices and electronic receivers, day after day, all across the land, the deserted speech of a statistical greed, summoning intelligence and materials out of the land to turn them into blights, justifying by an unearthly accounting and speech what decency would never have considered in the first place. There is no place that is not within reach of it and under threat of it. That speech is in Port William too, coming out of the walls of the houses, saying that all is well, all is better than ever, while the life of the place itself frets and fritters away in obedience to the omnivorous god of statistical probability. So that it becomes possible to foresee a human child as unrecognizable to its forebears as a new species, unable to recognize them, having no past that it has not forgotten, and no future or hope beyond the extrapolations of the general purpose.

By the time Andy and Flora returned from Chicago, the Port William schoolhouse had become a "rest home," where the old, use-less, helpless or unwanted sat like monuments, gaping into the oth-erworldly light of a television set. There, within two years of their return, Jarrat Coulter lay like a man carved on a tomb, only breath-ing, a forlorn contraption living on fluids needled into his veins. Andy would go from time to time, as the others did, and stand by his bed and gaze upon his wasting body, the derelict hands lying useless on the sheet. All of them went from time to time, duty bound, to stand beside him and watch him breathe indomitably on, and leave and never speak, to be troubled afterwards by what—whatever it was—they had not said.

Only Burley had the courage or the grace to make what seemed a visit. He did not stand by Jarrat and look. He went in and sat down as though invited to do so, and put his hat on his lap. And he talked. He talked without embarrassment either at his brother's silence or at the presence of whoever else might be there.

"Well, it looks like you're coming along all right. Comfortable, I'd say. You're just as well off here as you'd a been outside today. It's been a scorcher, I'll tell you. We put up a little jag of hay after dinner, me and the boys and the Rowanberrys. And it was just about all we wanted to do. When we got it all in, I said, 'Why don't we knock off the rest of the day? It's just too punishing hot.' They said all right, and the Rowanberrys went home, and the boys went off some-where—over to Nathan's, I *think*, and got some more work started there. I don't know, and to tell you the truth, I never asked. I went to the house and dragged my backyard chair over under the maple and set down. I've got several setting places now, Jarrat, and I go a right smart and set in them, and I don't feel bad about it. Course, that's because of the boys. They look after me and everything else pretty good. And Lyda looks after me when they don't."

He spoke into the silence where Port William's children had studied and played, and into Jarrat's silence. Sometimes, he would tell things that nobody on earth but Jarrat would have understood, if Jarrat was understanding them.

After he had said whatever Jarrat might be interested in hearing, he would get up and put on his hat. "Well, I've got to go. But I'll be back." He would lay his hand that was still brown and hard on his brother's pale, softening one. "Don't worry. You don't have to worry about a thing. Just rest and be easy in your mind."

In the river valley Andy takes the Port William road, and the pickup begins to move with a different motion, approaching the shape of the country. It moves now more nearly as eyes or feet might move, curving along the bases of the hills, not like a pencil point along the edge of a ruler. And Andy's body begins to live again in the familiar sways and pressures of his approach to home. His own place becomes palpable to him. Those he loves, living and dead, are no longer mere thoughts or memories, but presences, approachable and near.

He turns up Katy's Branch, going much slower now, following the road up along the creek in the shade of the overarching trees. He comes to his mailbox and turns into his own lane up Harford Run, the road hardly even a cut now but just a double track leveled along the valley side under the trees.

Now they are coming to him again, those who have brought him here and who remain—not in memory, but near to memory, in the place itself and in his flesh, ready always to be remembered—so that the place, the present life of it, resonates within time and within times, as it could not do if time were all that it is living in.

Now Mat runs up the bank toward Margaret, who is running to meet him with her arms open; they meet and hold each other at last.

Wheeler, standing on the bottom step of the coach as it sways and slows finally to a standstill at the station at Goforth, puts his hand into his father's hand and steps down.

Andy pushes open the door of the old house, and steps in behind Flora. They stop and stand looking at the wallpaper hanging in droops and scrolls, at the broken windowpane, at the phoebe's nest on the mantelpiece, and Flora says, "Oh, good!"

When he has driven up the slope in front of the house, and back alongside the house into the barn lot, and stopped the pickup in front of the barn, Andy switches off the engine, and sits still while the five-and-a-half-hour, two-thousand-mile uproar of his approach loosens from him and begins to withdraw like a long swarm of bees. When it has gone away, and the evening quiet of the place has returned to it and to him, he opens the door and gets out. An old black and white Border collie who has been standing beside the truck, waiting for him, now walks up and lifts his head under Andy's hand.

"You here all by yourself?"

The dog wags his tail appreciatively, and Andy strokes his head.

"Where is everybody?"

The evening chores, he sees, are done. The two jersey cows are loafing in the shade by the spring, their udders slack, and Flora's car is gone. He can hear the somnolent drumming of a woodpecker off in the woods, and from somewhere on the hillside above the barn the bleating of a sheep.

He takes his suitcase out of the cab and walks to the house and across the back porch, through the screen door, and into the kitchen, a pretty room, bright and quiet. He loves this quiet and he stands still in it, breathing it in. There is a note to him on the table; after looking at it for a minute or two, he goes over and reads it:

You're back?
Mart called. They have lots of beans.
We've gone to pick and visit.
            Love,
            F.

   With her note in his hand, standing in her place, in her absence,
he feels the strong quietness with which she has cared for him and
waited for him all through his grief and his anger. He feels her justice, her great dignity in her suffering of him. He feels around him a
blessedness that he has lived in, in his anger, and did not know. He
is walking now, from room to room, breathing in the smell of the
life that the two of them have made, and that she has kept. He walks
from room to room, entering each as for the first time, leaving it as
if forever. And he is saying over and over to himself, "I am blessed.
I am blessed."

   After a while he returns to the kitchen. He takes his suitcase to
his and Flora's bedroom and unpacks it and puts it away, and walks
again. He can no more sit down than if he has no knees. He does
not know when Flora and the children will be back, and he sees that
he cannot wait for them in the house. He puts on his work clothes
and starts out the back door. And then—the thought of mortality
returning to him; he must take no chance—he goes back to the
kitchen table and beneath Flora's note writes:

            Yes.
            I'm better now. Can you
            forgive me? I pray that you
            will forgive me.

The cows are still at the spring, still in the leisure of their drinking.
They look at him and look away, knowing him. To them he is no

one who has been far away, but only himself, whom they know, who is here. He takes a tin can from the ledge above the spring outlet and dips and drinks. And then he walks out into the pasture on the hillside.

The air is cooling now, the shadows growing long. He is walking upward along the face of the slope, following the slanting sodded groove of what was once a wagon road—before that perhaps a buffalo trace—that went from Katy's Branch to Port William. Where the road enters the woods, he opens a gate and goes through.

When he fenced the woods to keep the stock out, Elton asked him, "Why did you do that?"

"For the flowers," Andy said, giving one of his reasons.

Elton looked at him to see if he meant it. "Well. All right," he said.

The road slants on up through the woods, through the Harford Place and the others beyond, for perhaps a mile, staying as near as possible to Harford Run, until finally it comes out of the woods again on a high part of the upland near Port William.

The evening is quiet; there is no wind, and no sound from the stream that here, above the spring, is dry now. The woods is filling with shadows. Everything seems expectant, waiting for nightfall, though the sky is still sunlit. Andy walks slowly upward along the road until he is among the larger trees and the woods have completely enclosed him. And here finally he comes to rest. He finds a level place at the foot of a large white oak, and sits down, and then presently lies down. A heavy weariness has come over him. For a long time he has not slept a restful sleep, and he has journeyed a long way.

But the sleep that comes to him now is not restful. He has entered the dark, and it is such a darkness as he has never known. All that is around him and all that he is has disappeared into it. He sees nothing, remembers nothing, knows nothing except a hopeless longing for something he does not know, for which he does not know a name. Everything has been taken away, and the dark around him is full of the sounds of crying and of tearing asunder. If it is a sleep that he is in, he cannot awaken himself. Once he was nothing, and did not know it; and then, for a little while, it seems, he was something, to the sole effect that now he knows that he is nothing. And somewhere there is a lovely something, infinitely desirable, of which he cannot recall even the name. What he is, all that he is, amid the outcries in the dark and the rendings, is a nothing possessed of a terrible self-knowledge.

But now from outside his hopeless dark sleep a touch is laid upon his shoulder, a pressure like that of a hand grasping, and his form shivers and forks out into the darkness, and is shaped again in sense. Breath and light come into him. He feels his flesh enter into mind, mind into flesh. He turns, puts his knee under him, stands, and, though dark to himself, is whole.

He is where he was, in the valley, on the hillside under an oak, but the place is changed. It is almost morning and a gray light has made its way among the trees. The freshness of dew is on everything. And it is springtime, for the dry stream has begun to flow. The early flowers are in bloom, pale, at his feet. Everywhere, near and far away, there is birdsong. The birds sing a joy that is theirs and his, and neither theirs nor his.

When he has stood and looked around, he sees that a man, dark as shadow, is walking away from him up the hill road, not far ahead. Andy knows that, once, this man leaned and looked at him face to face and touched him, but now, walking ahead of him, is not going to look back.

He hurries to follow the dark man, who is almost out of sight and who he understands must be his guide, for the place, though it is familiar to him, is changed. Though he can see ahead to where his guide walks, the ground underfoot is dark, seeming not to exist until his foot touches it. He follows the dark man along the narrow ancient track in the almost dark, as when he was a boy he followed older hunters in the woods at night, Burley Coulter and Elton Penn and the Rowanberrys, men who knew the way, who, for all practical purposes, *were* the way of the places they led him through.

The trees on the hillside are large and old, as if centuries have passed since Andy was last here. It is growing rapidly lighter. Daylight is in the sky now, and against it, still in shadow, Andy can see the small new foliage of the great trees, the white and yellow and blue of the flowers, and birdsong fills the sky over the woods with a joy that welcomes the light and is like light.

And now above and beyond the birds' song, Andy hears a more distant singing, whether of voices or instruments, sounds or words, he cannot tell. It is at first faint, and then stronger, filling the sky and touching the ground, and the birds answer it. He understands presently that he is hearing the light; he is hearing the sun, which now has risen, though from the valley it is not yet visible. The light's music resounds and shines in the air and over the countryside, drawing everything into the infinite, sensed but mysterious pattern of its harmony. From every tree and leaf, grass blade, stone, bird, and beast, it is answered and again answers in return. The creatures sing back their names. But more than their names. They sing their being. The world sings. The sky sings back. It is one song, the song of the many members of one love, the whole song sung and to be sung, resounding, in each of its moments. And it is light.

He would stop, he would stop to stand and listen, or to stay forever, for he knows now that he has entered the eternal place in which we live in time, but the dark man, the dark man giving light, does not stop. He steps on up the hill road, and he does not look back.

Though the climb is longer than Andy remembers, even in its strangeness it is familiar. They go up beneath the great-girthed outspreading trees beside the stream of water coming down, the light glancing and singing off the little falls. As they climb, the music grows steadily stronger and brighter around them. The sun has come over the hill and is shining into the valley now. The shiver that stretched out in Andy's body when the dark man touched him has stayed in it. He is full of joy and he is afraid. He expects to die, and yet he lives, stepping on and on over the dry leaves and the little trembling flowers.

Finally the road brings them up, out from under the trees, onto the high part of the upland. And here the dark man does stop, and Andy stops, nearer to him than he has been before, but still several steps behind.

The dark man points ahead of them; Andy looks and sees the town and the fields around it, Port William and its countryside as he never saw or dreamed them, the signs everywhere upon them of the care of a longer love than any who have lived there have ever imagined. The houses are clean and white, and great trees stand among them and spread over them. The fields lie around the town, divided by rows of such trees as stand in the town and in the woods, each field more beautiful than all the rest. Over town and fields the one great song sings, and is answered everywhere; every leaf and flower and grass blade sings. And in the fields and the town, walking, standing, or sitting under the trees, resting and talking together in the peace of a sabbath profound and bright, are people of such beauty that he weeps to see them. He sees that these are the membership of one another and of the place and of the song or light in which they live and move.

He sees that they are the dead, and they are alive. He sees that he lives in eternity as he lives in time, and nothing is lost. Among the people of that town, he sees men and women he remembers, and men and women remembered in memories he remembers, and they do not look as he ever saw or imagined them. The young are no longer young, nor the old old. They appear as children corrected and clarified; they have the luminous vividness of new grass after fire. And yet they are mature as ripe fruit. And yet they are flowers. All of them are flowers.

He would go to them, but another movement of his guide's hand shows him that he must not. He must go no closer. He is not to stay. Grieved as he may be to leave them, he must leave. He *wants* to leave. He must go back with his help, such as it is, and offer it.

He has come into the presence of these living by a change of sight, by which he has parted from them as they were and from himself as he was and is.

Now he prepares to leave them. Their names singing in his mind, he lifts toward them the restored right hand of his joy.

Design by David Bullen
Typeset in Mergenthaler Sabon
by Wilsted & Taylor
Printed by Maple-Vail
on acid-free paper